N...
Ha...

romance
by Anne Mather
comes to life
on the movie screen

starring
KEIR DULLEA · SUSAN PENHALIGON

Leopard *in the* Snow

Guest Stars
KENNETH MORE · BILLIE WHITELAW

featuring GORDON THOMSON as MICHAEL
and JEREMY KEMP as BOLT

Produced by JOHN QUESTED and CHRIS HARROP
Screenplay by ANNE MATHER and JILL HYEM
Directed by GERRY O'HARA

An Anglo-Canadian Co-Production

Isle
of Desire

by

ANNE HAMPSON

Harlequin Books

TORONTO • LONDON • NEW YORK • AMSTERDAM • SYDNEY

Original hardcover edition published in 1977
by Mills & Boon Limited

ISBN 0-373-02130-5

Harlequin edition published January 1978

PRINTED IN U.S.A.

CHAPTER ONE

THE pale sun was setting behind the serrated line of tall buildings which stood out in all their stark ugliness against an April sky. High-rise flats. They formed a pattern of uneven concrete blocks behind the maze of factory buildings in the foreground. Casting a glance through the window, Laura Conroy frowned a little, then returned to her packing. Forty-eight hours from now she might be comfortably settled in a luxurious *palacio* on an island in the Tropics—or, far more probably, she could be on her way back home.

That she was practising deceit was an undoubted fact; whether or not she would get away with it remained to be seen.

One large suitcase was already in the hall; the one she was packing would soon join it. Both would accompany her first thing in the morning when the taxi came to take her to the airport.

Meanwhile, she had a date with her friend, Avice, who had insisted on taking her out to dinner, not because she was going away, but because she was today celebrating her twenty-fourth birthday.

After taking the suitcase to the hall Laura set about ticking off the numerous little jobs which of necessity had been left to the last. Her flat was being closed up; it would be reopened either in a couple of days' time, or in six months' time, depending on whether her deception would be condoned by the illustrious gentleman for whom she hoped to work.

The Conde Duarte André Volante de Taviro

Mauredo ... With a name like that he was bound to be illustrious, Avice had said with a grin. He would also be elderly, running to seed, and would probably be suffering from gout—or the modern equivalent—from over-indulgence in eating and drinking. He would be arrogant, full of his own importance because he owned an island.

'That kind never stops to think that it was their ancestors whom they've to thank for where they are,' Avice had continued, just as if she knew all about the man whose priceless paintings her friend was hoping to restore. 'You were telling me that this island of Torassa was purchased two centuries ago, and that the family of Mauredo had left Portugal to settle there after building themselves a magnificent palace?'

'That's right. The Conde explained all this in his first letter to my father.'

The first letter ... Laura was thinking about it as she bathed and dressed for the dinner at the Oaklands Hotel. In the letter the Conde had begun by saying he had had Mr Leonard Conroy's name given to him by a friend who had highly recommended his work. The Conde had then gone on to ask Mr Conroy if he would come over to the island and restore some paintings of his which required attention. The offer was accepted and Laura, who from the time of leaving the art school had assisted her father, had become excited at the prospect of living on a tropical island in the sun. The work would take about six months, the Conde had written, but he went on to say that time was not so important as a perfect result. And so if the work took twelve months it would be quite all right.

But long before Mr Conroy had made arrangements for the journey, another letter arrived with the information that the work would have to be postponed.

No reason was given; Laura had then gained the impression that anyone with a name like that of the Conde would consider it beneath his dignity to offer explanations to those whom he had been proposing to employ. A month after the arrival of this second letter Laura's father had had a heart attack and died. This was over eighteen months ago. The Conde had obviously not heard of Mr Conroy's death because, three weeks ago, he had written to say that the time was now convenient to him and he requested that Mr Conroy would come over as soon as possible and begin the restoration of the precious works of art. The letter, written in a purely businesslike manner, was addressed to L. Conroy, and it was while her eyes were focused on the initial that the daring idea was formulated in Laura's mind. Her own initial was L. More important, though, was the fact that she was an expert in her own right, having learned more from her father than she had at the art school where she had done so well.

She had replied to the Conde's letter, promising to arrive on the island in less than a month's time. She had signed her letter, L. Conroy.

Recollecting this as she took up a hairbrush from her dressing-table, Laura could not help smiling as she tried to picture the Conde's face when he saw who had arrived. Undoubtedly he would be taken aback, and it could transpire that he would order her to leave without even allowing her to show him the testimonials she carried, proving that she was capable of doing his work. It was a risk, but if it came off she would have the satisfaction of working on some very rare and beautiful paintings, and in addition she would have the pleasure of living in a palace.

The smile faded presently as she made a critical

7

examination of herself as she began to brush her hair. Shy, grey-green eyes which—so her father had always maintained—became moist and limpid when she smiled, stared back at her from the mirror. Her skin, of the transparent quality of fine china, required no make-up, nor did her lips. They were just like her mother's had been, her father used to say—'as red as ripe cherries'. Her manner had always been reserved and serious, her voice quiet and yet musical. A small sigh escaped her, for she was thinking of the way her father used to compare her with her mother. She wished she had known her, but Laura was only two years old when she died.

At last she put the brush down; her hair, a cascade of rich russet-brown, fell on to her shoulders, straight and shining and flicked up at the ends. A little perfume was sprayed upon it before, putting on an evening cloak of black velvet, Laura took up the sequin-trimmed bag and went out to the garage where she kept her car.

Half an hour later she was with her friend, in the hotel lounge, drinking an aperitif while waiting to be conducted to their table.

'Well, I expect the excitement's reaching fever pitch by now?' Avice smiled at Laura and added, 'I'm keeping my fingers crossed that this stuffy old Portuguese count will take you on.'

'I'm aware of the risk,' returned Laura frankly. 'It wouldn't surprise me if he orders me off the premises right away.'

'You might not get as far as entering them,' Avice warned. 'He's bound to be angry at being duped.'

Laura nodded in agreement. How humiliating it would be if she got no further than the front door! But that was not a logical thought, she instantly decided.

She must be invited into the palace—probably by a stiff forbidding butler who had been with the Conde for forty years or more.

'I must admit,' she mused, rather absently sipping her drink, 'that I'm beginning to feel a little apprehensive, now that the time for meeting the Conde is drawing near.'

'I can understand that,' was her friend's grim rejoinder. 'For my part, I'd have got cold feet long before now and written to tell him I couldn't come.'

'I would never do that. I want to see this island. It sounds intriguing. Just imagine one family owning a whole island!'

'It mightn't be very large.' Avice picked up her glass from the table. 'I don't suppose you know anything about his family? I mean, whether he has children or not?'

'I expect he has. These aristocrats who own property usually want an heir.'

Avice nodded her head.

'He'll probably have a tall angular wife who makes you feel like something that crawls, she's so superior. She'll wear diamonds no matter what time of day it is, and heavy gold necklaces and bracelets. She'll walk about the palace giving orders and stopping now and then to run a finger along the wainscoting to see if the maids have done the dusting properly.'

Laura laughed.

'We could be all wrong, you know. His wife might be charming.'

'Shouldn't think so. They're all snobs, those foreign aristocrats and their families. You'll find the children are so uppish they won't even look at you. No use going to that island with the romantic notion of attracting one of the Conde's sons. Their marriages will have

9

already been arranged for them—when they were about five years old, I shouldn't wonder.'

'I can assure you,' said Laura firmly, 'that I shan't be wasting my time on the Conde's sons. I'm going to restore pictures, not to run after someone who is obviously so far above me that his attention could never reach me anyway——' She stopped, and they both burst out laughing.

'Yes,' nodded Avice, 'I know. We're assuming all sorts of things that are probably wrong, and inventing people who might not exist.'

The waiter's appearance precluded any further discussion on the subject for a while. They were conducted to their table; the first course was served, and the wine.

'This is marvellous!' exclaimed Laura when presently the orchestra began playing quiet classical music. 'You've certainly made my birthday memorable. Thank you very much——' She was stopped by her friend's interruption,

'Don't thank me, Laura. I planned it some weeks ago, and I've really been looking forward to it. Your pleasure's no greater than mine.'

'Nevertheless,' returned Laura seriously, 'I must thank you.'

Avice merely smiled and a few moments later she and Laura were again discussing the appointment.

'Did he know just how well-known your father was in the art world?' Avice asked.

'I don't think so; someone had recommended him, certainly, but there was nothing in the Conde's letters to suggest that he had much knowledge at all about Father.'

Avice was frowning slightly.

'In that case, it's going to be very difficult indeed for you to convince him that you're capable of restoring these paintings. Had he known how great was your father's ability, then he might have taken more kindly to you, as his student.'

'I've thought of all that,' admitted Laura, 'and there's truth in what you're implying: he might refuse to believe that I'm capable of handling such precious works of art.'

'You do have your testimonials, though. Those should go some way to convincing him.'

'If he'll read them, of course.'

'Oh, well,' said Avice philosophically after a pause, 'you'll just have to wait and see. After all, you'll not have lost much even if he sends you packing.'

They both laughed, although Laura herself knew she would be bitterly disappointed if she were sent packing, as her friend termed it.

'Only my air fare,' she said.

The second course was brought and the conversation became more general. Then, with the meal over, they returned to the lounge for a final drink.

'To you—and your success on the island of Torassa!' Avice held up her glass. 'If any sincere wish of mine can bring you success, then success you most certainly shall have!'

The aeroplane was descending on to the island, an island that, even from the air, seemed characteristic of some fabulous terrain of a Disney film. Laura could see the Palacio, white against a background of several shades of green which she surmised to be made up of sweeping lawns, tropical shrubberies and exotic woodland surrounds. Colour came into focus; flower beds galore, then shapes which she deduced to be statuary. A fountain sparkled in the sunshine; a blue swimming-pool nestled among trees and shrubs and a rockery, from which water cascaded like threads of silver, into the pool.

Idyllic was the description that flashed into her mind. What a place to live! It seemed like fairyland, unreal, a place where heaven was just a breath away.

The aircraft rushed past the trees, then seemed to be stationary as it touched down and taxied to a smooth, almost imperceptible standstill. Laura was aware of bronzed faces, flashing smiles, leisurely movements. There seemed to be no hurry and scurry as she had known when landing at other airports.

A car was drawn up not far from the aircraft itself; Laura was later to learn that the Conde's chauffeur was quite used to driving up, close to the aircraft, whenever he had to meet either his employer or some visitor from abroad.

The uniformed man stood, looking rather blank as the last of the passengers alighted. Laura approached him and, smiling in the most winning way she knew, she inquired if he were here to pick up a certain L. Conroy. The man brightened and said yes, he was. Surprised that he should speak such excellent English, Laura said nothing for a moment and then, still smiling, she said that she was L. Conroy.

The man frowned at her and shook his head.

'I'm here to pick up an English gentleman,' he told her, his eyes scanning the tail-end of the passengers as they made their way towards the Customs shed.

'I have come in his place.'

'You?' The man stared at her disbelievingly. 'I think——'

'Will my luggage be through yet?' she interrupted. 'Perhaps you will see to it for me, and put in into the car?'

'But——'

'I assure you it will be all right,' said Laura, wishing she had as much confidence as she was endeavouring to display. 'The Conde is expecting me.'

'A gentleman,' said the man stubbornly.

'A lady,' she said and, without any more ado, she opened the door and got into the back of the car. To her relief she saw the man shrug his shoulders, and a few minutes later he was driving her off the landing-strip. Soon her luggage was in the car and they were on their way to the Palacio, passing through leafy lanes of exotic beauty before reaching a small town where smil-ing brown people waved gaily as the car sped along the main thoroughfare, its silver crest gleaming in the sunshine. Laura was so fascinated by her surroundings with their Eastern flavour that she was not for the present troubled by the apprehension that was slowly rising in her subconscious mind. But when eventually the car turned in through two high, exceedingly ornate wrought-iron gates, she forgot everything else but the meeting that was shortly to take place. The long curving drive was in reality another leafy lane, with lush green grass growing on either side, grass cut to look like a velvet carpet, soft and inviting to the feet. Flower beds blazing with colour provided the delight-ful patterns with which the green carpet was strewn. Looking beyond the tall trees which backed the wide verges, Laura saw the palace setting—sweeping lawns, a cascading fountain making rainbows in the sun, ter-races blazing with colour, statues holding lamps which, she surmised, were lighted at night. In the distance was a shining lake overhung with trees; on its smooth waters aquatic plants sent forth a blaze of colour and, swimming about among them, were brightly-plumaged birds. On the bank several peacocks preened them-selves, while the less colourful peahens looked on.

Then came the house itself, and Laura gave a little gasp as she took in its beauty and its size. White, like marble, its porphyry-encrusted façade forming the only real contrast, the great palace was a superlative example of an eighteenth-century *senhorial* house such as could be seen in Portugal itself. It had lacy Gothic-style windows and balconies, and many richly-sculptured embellishments including great white columns around which grew bougainvillaea vines in various colours.

The car swung into a wide curve before coming to a smooth halt in front of a flight of marble steps flanked by huge stone vases containing Traveller's Palms.

The chauffeur got out and opened the door for her. She stepped from the car, her mind now becoming dazed by all the splendour of her surroundings. An emerald humming-bird darted past her, barely a couple of feet from her face, and flew to a nearby bush of vivid scarlet flowers. Another flash of colour was made by a parakeet flitting about among the delicate blue flowers of a jacaranda tree. Behind her the door opened, jerking her mind back to stark reality and the knowledge that, within the matter of a few minutes, she could be getting back into the car.

She turned, almost reluctantly, lifting an unsteady hand to remove a tendril of russet hair from her eyes. Her heart was beating far too quickly for comfort, and something intangible was affecting her breathing.

A butler stood there, not the ancient retainer whom she and Avice had invented, but a smart, square-shouldered young man of about thirty years of age. His face, unsmiling, was brown, his hair black. She saw his eyes move to the stolid-faced chauffeur, an expression of inquiry in their depths. Words passed between the two, but as they spoke in Portuguese Laura had no idea what was being said.

'I have come instead of my father,' she decided to explain as soon as the men stopped talking. 'I trust the Conde will see me.' For a moment she thought the butler did not understand her language, so impassive was his face. However, he moved aside, allowing her to enter the massive hall which was hung with tapestries of exquisite workmanship and design. Weapons of all kinds decorated the panelled walls of this light and airy apartment where flowers predominated. They grew in pots which were themselves encased in urns of gleaming silver, bronze and copper.

'Dom Duarte is indeed expecting a gentleman,' said the butler in excellent English. 'I will inform him of your arrival.'

'Dom Duarte?' she frowned. 'Isn't it the Conde whom I'm to meet?'

The man portrayed surprise, but only for a few seconds.

'It is correct for you to address the Conde as Dom Duarte,' he said, and the trace of a smile came to his lips. 'In Portugal, and of course here on Torassa, Dom is in itself a title.'

'I see ...' Not for the life of her could she imagine herself using the Conde's Christian name, but of course she did not say anything to the butler, merely moving towards an open door which he was indicating, the flick of his hand an invitation for her to enter.

'If you will wait there, I will be back directly.'

He was not back directly, and by the time she did see him enter the room where she was sitting, she had convinced herself that the Conde had decided not to see her at all, but to give instructions for her to be taken back to the airport immediately.

However, the butler was ready to show her to the room where the Conde was waiting. She entered, feeling very small and shy and inadequate, overawed even before her eyes had encountered the Conde himself. For the room, high-ceilinged and elegantly furnished with settees and armchairs covered in deep blue velvet with gold trimmings, was the most magnificent she had ever seen. The ceiling was painted in exquisite colours, its scenes depicting historical events in the history of Portugal. The carpet was Persian, the occasional furniture of rosewood, and beautifully carved. All this she absorbed in a flash, but she had the added impression of luxurious cushions, long velvet drapes, silver ornaments and light fittings, beautiful antique porcelain, and much more besides, all of which combined to create an atmosphere of elegance and good taste.

And then she saw the man, standing with his back to the high wide fireplace, and a little gasp of surprise escaped her. Could this be the Conde?

About thirty years of age, tall and straight with lean aristocratic features and a head of healthy black hair, he was very far removed from the picture that she and Avice had invented, which was that of an elderly man with a stoop and a paunch, and perhaps a bald head. His eyes were of a dark metallic grey, with lazy lids which were now half closed, narrowing his eyes to little more than slits; his nose had an aquiline quality which, combined with the high cheekbones, gave a sort of satanic appearance to his face. The mouth, firm but not thin, had a hint of sensuousness about it which seemed out of keeping with the general impression of cold hauteur which his manner gave.

He was looking her over with a sort of quelling arrogance; she gained the impression that his mind was almost made up and she would not have been in the least surprised to hear him order her off the premises without even giving her a hearing. However, he did no such thing, but inquired about her father, adding that his butler had informed him that she had come in his stead.

'I don't quite understand, *senhorita*,' he added, 'but no doubt you will explain?' His accent was alien and abrupt, but courteous for all that. 'Sit down, if you please—— No, not there. Here.' His gesture was imperious as he indicated a chair that faced the full flow of light coming through one of the floor-to-ceiling windows; it was plain that he meant to watch her closely as she spoke, which to Laura was more than a little disconcerting even before she opened her mouth.

'Had my father carried out the commission which you originally gave him,' she began, lifting her shy eyes to his, 'I would have accompanied him here, as I've worked for him for some considerable time.' She stopped for a moment, her discomfiture increasing rapidly under his cool, unsmiling stare. 'I have testimonials to prove my own efficiency,' she went on, but he interrupted her, a faint frown creasing his forehead.

'Your father, *senhorita*, you haven't explained why he isn't here?'

She bit her lip, finding herself quite unable to speak as freely and unreservedly as she had intended. But then this young and coolly autocratic nobleman was far more disconcerting than she had expected. In any case, she had come prepared to see someone much older and, therefore, perhaps more mellowed and tolerant. This man's eyes were hard, like steel, his air one of superiority and detachment; she had felt at a disadvantage from the first moment of setting eyes on him.

'The commissions which were outstanding——'

'*Senhorita*,' interrupted the Conde sharply, 'I want to know why your father isn't here!'

She coloured swiftly, and averted her head.

'He died eighteen months ago,' she answered in a quiet, rather hopeless little voice. She might just as well make her departure at once, she thought, because she was gaining nothing by remaining here, waiting for the Conde to dismiss her from his august presence.

'Died?' repeated the Conde disbelievingly. 'And you have come here, expecting to take his place?'

She nodded her head, swallowing saliva that was collecting in her mouth.

'I'm very capable, sir. I have testimonials here, in my handbag—if—if you would be so kind as to take a look at them? As I was about to say a moment ago,' she went on perseveringly, 'the commissions outstanding at my father's death were taken over by me and have been executed to the complete satisfaction of the people concerned.' As she had been speaking she had withdrawn a large envelope from her bag, but she did not offer it to him, for his expression restrained her from doing so.

'Am I to understand, *senhorita*, that you have come here expecting to work on my pictures?' His voice held an incredulous note; his brilliant dark eyes held censure.

'I'm capable of doing so——' She stopped and looked questioningly at him. 'Your butler said it was correct for me to address you as Dom Duarte?'

The Conde inclined his dark head.

'It will be quite in order for you to use that form of address.'

'Well,' she began again awkwardly, 'as I was saying, I'm capable of working on your paintings, as you will agree once you have read my testimonials—that is,' she added, deliberately injecting an encouraging edge to her voice, 'if you would be so obliging as to take a look at them?' She automatically took up the envelope, but again replaced it on top of her handbag, for the Conde was shaking his head.

'My paintings are far too valuable for me to take any risks about their restoration.' There was no mistaking the implacable note to the foreign, urbane voice, and once again Laura lost hope. 'Might I ask your age?' he added.

'I'm twenty-four,' she replied.

The Conde lifted his straight black brows in a gesture that made her feel like a child of five years of age.

'Twenty-four, and you boast of your experience in the world of art?' The tinge of mocking amusement in the Conde's voice seemed strangely out of place, discouraging though it was. Up till now he had displayed only hauteur; the fact that he could be amused seemed to make him a little more human. Nevertheless, he had caused her to colour up as embarrassment made itself felt. And because of this embarrassment, she also felt angry. He was an arrogant and pompous man to assume that, because she was young, she was not capable of working on his precious paintings.

'I wasn't boasting,' she retorted. 'I was merely stating a fact. I shall state that fact again, Dom Duarte. I *am* capable of handling those paintings.'

The deep grey eyes glinted, and there was now a certain ruthlessness about his mouth which Laura had not noticed before. She found herself examining his face more closely, discovering that the lines which she had mentally described as obdurate could in fact spell cruelty, that the out-thrust jawline could denote a mercilessness rather than the mere quality of firmness which was her first impression. And yet she had to own to the superlative good looks which the Conde possessed; he was the most handsome man she had ever encountered.

19

'Perhaps you are capable,' came the Conde's surprising comment at last, 'but even if you are, do you suppose I'd condone the deceit you have practised on me?'

'The letter you sent was addressed to L. Conroy ...' Laura tailed off to silence, aware even before encountering the severity in his eyes that she was being absurd.

'You knew to whom the letter was addressed, *senhorita*. It was incumbent on you to write to me, informing me of the death of the man I had commissioned to do my work, and offering your own services in place of his.'

'Would you even have considered my offer?' she challenged, her shy, grey-green eyes looking directly into his.

'I believe I might have looked more kindly on such an offer than I can on this deception.' He searched her face intently before adding, 'Tell me, *senhorita*, just why did you practise this deceit?'

'I thought that, if I wrote to you saying Father had died, you'd then have cancelled the commission.'

'So it was to have been a *fait accompli*?' His black brows were raised, his head shaking from side to side, slowly. 'It was a great pity you didn't know me, *senhorita*, for then you would not have acted so unwisely.'

She nodded unhappily.

'You won't give me a trial, then?'

The Conde shook his head.

'Not under the circumstances. Firstly, there's the deceit, and secondly, there's the doubt in my mind about your ability to restore my paintings to my entire satisfaction. I'm a perfectionist, and therefore I desire a perfectionist to do the work for me. That is the reason I sent for your father.'

'But I've worked with him, Dom Duarte. No one has ever found fault with my work.'

20

'Perhaps the pictures you've restored are not so valuable as mine.'

Laura's chin shot up; it was on the tip of her tongue to inform this arrogant nobleman that she had titled people among her clients. However, she was quelled by his expression and merely said, in her low and musical voice,

'If you would look at my testimonials, Dom Duarte, you would—I think—be most impressed by the names of the people who wrote them.'

'Most probably,' he agreed in his clipped and alien accents. 'However, I am a busy man, *senhorita*, and never spend my time unproductively. Therefore I shall, I'm afraid, be denied the pleasure of reading what these illustrious clients of yours have written about you.' He was rising as he spoke and she knew she was being dismissed. Humiliation and anger replaced that shy expression in her eyes and for a long moment the Conde stood taking this in until, a quality of shrewdness entering his voice, he asked her why it had seemed so important that she should come to Torassa.

'I have a strong suspicion,' he continued before she could reply, 'that it was the idea of a few months' sojourn in a tropical island that was the incentive, rather than a keen and sincere desire to do some useful work.'

It was seldom that Laura's temper was strained to the point where she failed to control it, but she was very close to that point now. Her eyes glinted, almost after the fashion of the Conde's, a few minutes previously. She stood up, small beside his towering figure, but what she lacked in height she made up for in courage and pride. With great dignity she said,

'I can see that there is no purpose in continuing this interview. If you would be so obliging as to have your

21

chauffeur drive me to the airport I should be most grateful. I did not notice as I came away, but I expect there's an hotel there where I might stay for tonight?'

'Tonight, *senhorita*? There is no flight tomorrow.'

'Oh ...' A frown touched her clear high forehead. 'When is there a flight, then?'

'Not for another week. There is no flow of air traffic to this island. We like to retain our privacy as much as we can.'

So he must keep his island to himself, she thought. What he ought to have been was a feudal lord, living in the Middle Ages! She could quite easily imagine him riding arrogantly through his lands, finding fault with the poor peasants over whom he ruled—and probably ordering them to be thrown into a dungeon, or flogged and put through some other kind of torture.

'I shall just have to wait, then. This hotel——'

'Does not exist,' he broke in suavely. 'There is no necessity for one on Torassa, since we never admit tourists. The only visitors we have are friends or business acquaintances; these naturally are accommodated by the people they have come to see.'

What a strange place! And yet on second thoughts she could admit that it was idyllic. A sun-drenched island in the tropics which the inhabitants were able to keep entirely to themselves. No intruders searching for land to use for hotel building, no holiday flats, no funfairs or gaudy souvenir stalls. Just what nature provided—the white sandy beaches, the lush vegetation, the brightly-plumaged birds ... and the Lord of the Manor to keep order.

Laura gave a deep sigh, thinking of what might have been could she have persuaded this man to allow her to work on his pictures.

'You sigh,' he observed, and she could not be sure

whether or not there was a flicker of mockery in his steely grey eyes. 'Is it disappointment at not being able to stay here, on the island, for six months or so, or is it annoyance that there is no flight for a week?'

She moved uncomfortably. His perception annoyed her as much as it surprised her. Yet she found herself saying, with a frankness she had not meant to betray,

'I must admit, Dom Duarte, that the prospect of spending a few months on a tropical island did lend enhancement to the idea of doing your work for you.' She was looking up into his face, her customary manner of seriousness and reserve strongly to the fore. 'What am I to do about leaving? Is there a boat I could take?'

For a long moment the Conde remained silent, staring down at her, examining her expression as if analysing it thoroughly. For some reason she smiled, and her eyes took on that liquid radiance which her father had always found so enchanting, and invariably remarked upon, saying it reminded him of her mother. The Conde's metallic eyes flickered and he appeared to be deep in thought. But at length he said, coolly, but not in those clipped accents which gave his English a rather unusual sound,

'I commend you on your honesty, *senhorita*. Had you denied being disappointed at not being able to remain here, I should have known you were lying. However, you told the truth. As for a boat——' He shook his head. 'You will be accommodated here at the Palacio until a week today——'

'Oh, but——'

'During that time, *senhorita*, if you and I do come into conversation, you will kindly *not* interrupt me. I'm unused to such lack of respect from those around me. I hope I make myself clear?'

She had coloured hotly at the rebuke, and as her temper was almost at breaking point she would have derived extreme satisfaction from telling him what she thought about him. She did nothing of the kind, though, being conscious of her obligation to him in being forced to accept his hospitality.

'Yes, Dom Duarte,' she said meekly at last, 'you do make yourself clear. I am sorry for the interruption.'

'Where is your luggage?' he asked. 'Is it still in the car?'

'I don't know,' she had to admit. 'It was in the boot, but the chauffeur might have taken it out.'

'In that case it will be in the hall——' He reached up to pull on a long bell-rope made of fine gold wire twisted into an intricate pattern and ending in a loop. 'We shall soon see,' he told her. 'If you are ready one of my maids will be here directly to take you to your room.'

CHAPTER TWO

THE room to which Laura was shown was perfection in its sheer simplicity of taste and colour. The walls were of pale lilac, the drapes of white to match the thick-pile carpet and the fine hand-embroidered bedspread. The suite was of fine sandalwood; the headboard of quilted velvet was of pale lilac, as were the chair and the stool in front of the dressing-table. Laura, thrilled with it all, had a second surprise on being shown the bathroom, which was also in white and pale lilac.

'Martim is bringing up your suitcase, *senhorita*.' The maid, whose name was Teresa, smiled as she mentioned the chauffeur's name. Laura was to learn that the couple were engaged to be married. 'Would you wish me to unpack for you?'

'No, thank you all the same.' Laura looked faintly puzzled. 'Do you all speak English?' she inquired.

'Most people here speak English, *senhorita*. You see, Torassa was once owned by an Englishman who brought many servants and friends here. The friends left when my master's family bought the island from the Englishman, but the servants remained. They have married with the original natives, and so we are this colour——' She pointed to her cheek and laughed. 'It is nice, don't you think?'

'Very attractive,' returned Laura, smiling. 'The Conde, though, he is pure Portuguese?'

'Of course. He owns many estates in Portugal, and vineyards; from these he makes his money.'

'But lives permanently here, on Torassa?'

'That is right. Dom Duarte is a lover of peace and quietness. He is glad that his people of the past decided to buy this island. It is a very beautiful island, yes?'

'I haven't seen much of it at all yet. I saw the lovely beaches from the air, and some high land in the interior.'

'We have mountains in the middle of our island, with beautiful trees growing there and pretty streams starting their life.'

Pretty streams starting their life ... What a poetical way of putting it, thought Laura, smiling at the girl.

'I hope I shall be able to go up and see some of these streams,' she said.

'If you are Dom Duarte's guest then of course he will see that you are shown everything. He is an excellent host, as you will soon discover.' The maid glanced around. 'If there is nothing else, *senhorita*, then I will go?'

'There's nothing else, thank you.'

The girl departed and a few moments later the luggage had been brought up. Laura hesitated about unpacking all her things, but then she decided to do so, as her dresses and blouses would be better in the wardrobe than in the cases, even if the majority of them were never worn while she was on the island. A week ... so short a time, and yet, in a way, she was fortunate. Had there been a flight she would never have had any opportunity at all of seeing the island. As it was, she decided she would take what was offered and try to have an enjoyable week's holiday on this paradise island upon whose shores tourists were not allowed.

After unpacking she had a bath, then changed into slacks and an open-necked shirt-blouse. She wanted to explore the grounds of the Palacio de Mauredo, then proceed to the Great Park which surrounded it. After that, if she still had time before dark, she would make her way to the shore. She wondered about her food and if she would eat with the servants. She supposed she would, and this supposition naturally led to the question: what would the servants think about her? They would soon have learned that she had been refused the work which she had hoped to do, would know that her deceit had definitely not met with the Conde's approval.

She shrugged inwardly, deciding it was unprofitable to dwell on such things. She had known from the first that what she proposed doing was a gamble. Well, it had not come off, and the venture had been a loss financially, since she had to pay her own air fare, which would not have been the case had she been able to carry out the commission. However, so long as she was having to pay her fare, she might as well have something for it. A week on the lovely island of Torassa would be an experience she would not forget for a long time to come.

Her room had a balcony and Laura stepped out on to it, her appreciative eyes wandering over the lovely scene of part of the Palacio gardens where exotic flowers spread their incredible colours between areas of smooth green lawns. A fountain shot its spray towards the clear blue crystal sky; its waters, penetrated by sunshine, flashed every colour of the rainbow as they fell back into the lily pool from which they had emerged. Statues looked down upon another pool, which was lined with precious azulejos and into whose waters dipped the branches of willows growing along one side of it. At the other side was a terraced rose garden, while at both ends were shady bowers in which were brightly-coloured garden chairs.

A sigh escaped Laura; it was a mingling of pleasure and disappointment.

'I wish it were six months,' she said in a whisper. 'But never mind; at least I have a week.'

A few minutes later she was in the garden, walking slowly from one delectable bush to another and wondering how she could discover their names. Of the trees she recognised the fragrant frangipani with its thick glossy leaves and creamy white flowers, the Royal poinciana and the tropical Flame of the Forest. A slender allamanda spread a shower of delicate gold as it climbed all over the stump of a dead tree which had been left there specifically for the plant to use for its support.

Wandering on, Laura strolled past more colourful borders, trod wide paths between lawns, came upon little waterfalls and rock gardens, all basking in the warm sunshine of this quiet, enchanting island floating like a jewel in the tropical waters of the Indian Ocean.

How lucky the Conde was!—and all who lived here, for that matter. Those who worked for him seemed to be inordinately happy and contented. Laura shrugged away the access of regret which would have intruded into the pleasure she was deriving from her stroll. The sun on her face, the breeze from the sea teasing her hair, the flower perfumes assailing her nostrils ... all these compounded to vanquish any dampness of spirit she might otherwise have experienced.

Half an hour later she was in the Great Park, gasping over and over again at the beauty of the trees and shrubs. Here again were clumps of frangipani trees, some the lovely white which she had already seen, but some were bright red, making an impressive contrast to the gold of the dhak trees growing close by. The orange flowers of the flamboyant trees made another contrast, this time with the dark green foliage of the Chinese fan palms and the paler green of the beautiful mountain tallows. The ground beneath these trees was covered with a myriad varieties of low plants, all brightly-coloured, while in the branches of some of the tall trees could be seen orchids of many subtle colours and shapes.

Suddenly Laura tensed, aware of some slight sound disturbing the utter stillness and serenity of the Park. She turned her head, then stopped, wondering if her colour had heightened, as she felt it had. The Conde, dressed in white slacks and a white shirt, open at the throat and with the sleeves rolled up above the elbows, had come into the Park and was approaching her with the long easy strides of an athlete. He reached her and she found herself stammering as she asked if he minded her being here.

'Of course not.' His voice was the courteous one which he had at first used and she surmised that he was not going to mention her deceit again. She was not forgiven, of course, but neither was she to be reminded of her wrongdoing. She managed a smile as she thanked him, then ventured to comment on some of the wonders she had seen since coming out more than an hour ago.

'I've never even imagined such beauty,' she added, 'much less been fortunate enough to see it, and walk among it. Your gardens leave me breathless, Dom Duarte.'

The cold eyes remained expressionless, so that she could not discover whether or not her words had pleased him. What an aloof man he was! As she looked up into his face she thought: I might be looking at one of those stone statues over there, in the garden.

'You must enjoy whatever my house and gardens offer,' he said urbanely at last. 'As you have to be here, then obviously you'll want to make the most of your visit.'

'Yes, that's how I look at it.' Her smile fluttered; she saw his own eyes move with the merest flicker. 'Thank you for saying I may enjoy what your house has to offer. I'm interested in antiques, naturally, and I shall love looking around. I know I shall be especially interested in the pictures——' She stopped, having spoken without thinking. The Conde seemed to smile faintly and again there was a hint of a flicker in his eyes.

'Naturally you will be interested in my pictures,' he agreed in tones of sardonic amusement. 'Most of them are in the gallery, which you will find on the first floor of the Palacio.'

'Thank you.' She wished she could feel more at ease— or, alternately, that he would leave her. She was puzzled as to why he was here, but dared not ask him. However, he explained within the next few seconds and she learned that, in the Great Park, there was a swimming-pool and something had gone wrong with its drainage system.

'I should have thought you would have someone do it for you,' she said, for the second time not stopping to think.

'I certainly do not intend to fix drains myself,' was the curt reply she received before, with a slight inclination of the head, the Conde went on his way.

Laura stood where he had left her, biting her lip and angrily asking herself why she had spoken out of turn, not once only, but twice. She felt awkward in his company, that was the crux of the matter. His cold austerity, his arrogance and superiority, the memory of her own act of deceit which had brought her here in the first place—all these contributed in part to her lack of composure when in his presence. She wondered if her stay on this lovely coral island was going to be all rosy and pleasant after all.

It was half past seven that evening. She had watched from her balcony as the sun went down—a brilliant red disc hovering at the horizon's edge, its fiery rays mirrored in the tranquil sea. Closer to, in the vast grounds of the Palacio, trees had been dappled with gold and saffron and flame, while the mountainsides in the far distance to the north of the island were already shadowed in duns and greys as the sky above them paled to turquoise before swiftly deepening to indigo, then to the deep purple through which the brightening stars appeared. The dusk had been beautiful, like a spreading haze of soft and gentle colour advancing on the last gilded rays that glowed from the dying light of the sun. And now the air was sweet and fresh; moths had appeared, and the chirping of crickets mingled with the croaking of frogs and the occasional call of a monkey or a night bird.

Laura had changed into a dress but had not taken any special care with her appearance. She had walked for miles since coming to the island that morning and she was tired—almost ready for bed, in fact, and had she not felt so hungry she most certainly would have turned in.

She was about to make her way down to the kitchen, which she had located earlier, from outside, when there was a gentle tap on her door and Teresa opened it in response to Laura's 'come in'.

'Dom Duarte asked me to tell you that dinner will be served at half past eight in the small dining-room.'

Laura blinked.

'He means that I am to dine with him?' she queried in surprise.

'That's right, *senhorita*.' Teresa's dark eyes made a swift and surreptitious examination of Laura's attire. 'It is customary for guests to dress for dinner,' she murmured tactfully but with a smile. 'Will you need my help at all?'

Laura smiled and shook her head.

'No, thank you, Teresa.' A slight pause and then, 'The small dining-room—is that it, next to the Blue Lounge?'

'No, that's Dom Duarte's private sitting-room. I think I had better show you the small dining-room; it's rather out of the way.'

A few moments later Laura was being shown the room, after having been taken through the large front hall, along a thickly-carpeted corridor into a side hall, and it was off this that the small dining-room was situated. Laura thanked the girl, then went back to her bedroom. She had managed to hide her apprehension from Teresa, but it had been there, for all that. Now, she realised, her heart was beating much too quickly and in a vague sort of way she was searching for an excuse not to dine with the Conde. A headache? Not convincing at all. She was tired? Again not convincing, seeing that it was still early evening. Laura sighed, aware that whatever excuse she could think up would carry no real weight. The Conde would know it was not genuine.

Resignedly accepting that she must dine with him, Laura examined her wardrobe for what she thought would be most suitable. She chose a simple outfit in the end—a plain black velvet skirt and a white lacy blouse with long sleeves and a neckline that fitted snugly to her throat.

The Conde, looking superlative in an off-white linen suit with frilled shirt and a black bow-tie, was standing by the long low window, looking out on to a scene of statuary and fountains, of terraces and parterres, all floodlit with lights of varying colours—soft yellows, rose pinks, gentle greens and mauves. He turned on hearing her soft footfall as she entered the room, and his grey eyes looked her over appraisingly. She coloured delicately, forcing a smile, which brought that limpid radiance to her lovely eyes. The Conde held a glass in his hand; he politely inquired if she would like a drink.

'No, thank you,' she returned shyly.

'Do sit down,' he invited. 'Over here, on the window seat. Dinner will be about ten minutes or so.'

She sat down, feeling small and very much out of her element. She spoke, voicing what was in her mind.

'I was surprised to receive your invitation to dine with you. I had expected to eat in the kitchen.'

The Conde's steely eyes opened wide.

'In the kitchen?' he repeated. 'What on earth gave you an idea like that?'

'If I had entered your employ, then I'd have expected to eat with the servants.'

'You would not have been that kind of a servant.' He emptied his glass and placed it on the sideboard. 'I had considered your father as an artist, working on his own account. I would never have thought of him as an employee of mine, but rather as a business associate who was doing me a service.'

Laura said, after a little hesitant pause,

'I am capable of doing that service, sir. My father taught me all he knew——'

'But could not give you the experience that comes

33

with age, *senhorita*.' The smooth finality of this precluded any further attempts at persuasion on Laura's part, and she resolved never to mention the paintings again.

An awkward pause was avoided by the Conde asking about her afternoon's perambulations.

'After strolling round the gardens here, and the Great Park, I went to the shore and walked along there for miles.' She looked up at him from her seat in the window; he was not so very far away and she could smell the faintly perceptible fragrance of an aftershave lotion. 'The beach is lovely. I've never seen white sands before ...' She tailed off, pleasantly recalling the palms against the southern sky, swaying gently in the breeze drifting in from the coral sea. The waves washed, so gently, against the shore. Small boats could be seen, far out on the smooth waters, their brightly-coloured sails flapping in the breeze. She saw a surf-rider, and a couple of para-gliders, but the people on the beach could be counted on her hands. 'Nor have I been on a beach with so few people on it.'

'Our population is extremely low here,' returned the Conde in his distant, aristocratic manner. 'This, and the entire absence of tourists, keeps our island as near as possible, in its original state. We have to build houses, but you will have noticed that they are thatched for the most part with palm leaves. Our roads are kept down to a minimum, so that it is possible to walk in the countryside undisturbed by the noise and dust of traffic. On the island are many kinds of terrain. We have some mountainous country, some level arable land, some terraced vineyards and even some jungle.'

'It sounds fascinating.' Her voice was low, her eyes dreamy. She had no idea just how attractive she was at this moment, or how appealing her manner. She turned her head automatically, to take in the wonders of the gardens behind her, gardens which, being a combination of what prodigal nature could produce, and the great care and attention given by dedicated men employed by the Conde, were the very acme of perfection. A small sigh escaped her; she thought of her father, wishing he had lived to enjoy the six months or more on Torassa which would have been necessary had he taken on the work of restoring the paintings. The Conde's quiet, foreign voice came to her, penetrating her thoughts but not dispersing them.

'You will have to explore as much of Torassa as you can in the short time you have. I will have someone at your service, if you so wish, who will take you around.'

She turned to glance up into his mahogany dark face, a sudden smile appearing, and with it that limpid moisture which made her beautiful eyes even more arresting. The Conde's attention was caught; his dark eyes flickered, then moved, in a slow examination of her features—the high unlined forehead and curving eyebrows, the thick curling lashes which threw enchanting shadows on to her pale, clear-skinned cheeks. He noticed the firm little chin, pointed so that it gave the effect of an elfin quality, the youthful curves beneath the lacy blouse, the narrow waist, the slender ankles, revealed because her legs were crossed, thus bringing the velvet skirt away from the floor.

'That is kind of you, Dom Duarte,' she said shyly. 'It will be a great help if I have with me someone who knows the island.'

'Would you prefer a man or a woman?'

She gave a start of surprise. Aware of the strictness of the Portuguese nobility regarding morals, she had not expected to be given a choice of this kind.

'I expected you would have given me a woman,' she said, speaking her thoughts aloud.

'Had you been my sister,' he returned, 'then most certainly you would have had a woman accompany you. However, in your country it is different and, therefore, I give you the choice.'

She said quietly, without even pausing to consider,

'Could I have Teresa?'

The merest smile touched his noble mouth.

'Already you like her? Teresa has always been popular. Martim is envied by all his unmarried friends.' The Conde nodded his head. 'Yes, have Teresa by all means. She will, I expect, welcome an off-duty period like this.'

Laura looked at him, examining him in a new light. He seemed quite willing to give Teresa a week off from her duties in the Palacio; he had also spoken of her with a touch of admiration in his voice. Laura searched his face for a sign of softness, of real humanity. She saw only hard eyes like steel, a firm out-thrust jaw, an implacable mouth. Did he ever unbend, this aristocrat with the air of a feudal lord?

'Thank you,' she murmured, suddenly aware that he was waiting for some comment from her. 'It will be far more pleasant to explore the island with Teresa than by myself.'

The dinner was soon served and, sitting opposite to Dom Duarte at the small table, Laura was amazed to discover that she was at ease. She had dreaded the meal, had assured herself that it would be a strain and that she would give a deep sigh of relief when it was over and she could escape to her room, away from the awe-inspiring presence of the Conde Duarte André Volante de Taviro Mauredo. Instead she was—perhaps subconsciously—wanting the meal to be prolonged, for the conversation, hinging on antiques and various well-known works of art, was naturally as interesting to Laura as it was to her noble host. For his part, he several times betrayed his surprise at her knowledge, and when at length the meal was over and they retired to the Blue Lounge for coffee and liqueurs she felt sure his opinion of her had risen since the first uncomfortable meeting only that morning.

The coffee was brought on a gleaming silver tray, carried in by Gigo, an immaculately-attired manservant. His dark eyes slid to Laura, but only for a second.

'You can leave the tray,' said the Conde in English. 'We will serve ourselves.'

However, once the man had gone Dom Duarte himself poured Laura's coffee, and then his own. She watched his slender brown hands, noting their strength, and she gained the extraordinary impression that they could be infinitely gentle, this in spite of their appearance of iron-hardness and the idea that they could inflict the direst pain and cruelty on anyone who was unwise enough to arouse in their owner the primitive instincts which Laura was certain he possessed. Conscious of her intensive stare, Dom Duarte stopped in the act of passing her the sugar and his straight black brows lifted a fraction in a gesture of arrogant inquiry. She coloured adorably in her embarrassment, looked down into her cup of steaming coffee, and waited for him to speak.

'Is something wrong, *senhorita*?' The alien voice, cold as ice, plunged Laura into an inexplicable feeling of dejection. It was as if this change in his manner had spoiled the whole evening.

'No—no, of course not,' she stammered. 'Why should you ask?'

'The way you were staring at me,' was his reply. And then, unexpectedly, 'Tell me, *senhorita*, what were you thinking about?'

She glanced at his hands, one of which was now picking up the silver cream jug.

'It was nothing important, Dom Duarte.' She managed to bring back the steadiness to her voice, managed to look directly at him as she spoke. 'Just mind-wanderings, if you know what I mean?' she added with a light laugh.

The cream was passed to her in silence; she felt reproved by his deliberate lack of response to what she had said. The next time the Conde spoke it was to ask which liqueur she preferred. She told him and he poured it for her, still maintaining his reproving silence. However, Laura herself managed to reopen the conversation and the gathering tension was eased, much to her relief. They talked again of antiques, and to her surprise the Conde offered to show her some very special pieces which he had bought when in China a couple of years previously.

'They're Celadons,' he explained after conducting her to the room in which the precious pieces were housed. 'Their period—the Sung Dynasty.'

Laura had seen Celadons before; she knew they were of the period between the tenth and thirteenth centuries, a period in China when cultural and creative achievements were at their peak. The beautiful things that had been made at that time had more than once left Laura breathless.

However, for some reason she could not explain, she made no mention of her previous experience of these beautiful examples of delicate china, but merely enthused on their colour, their shape, and the fact that they had survived for at least seven centuries. Her appreciation was noted, but she gained the rather disconcerting impression that, somehow, she had made a slip, revealing the fact that she was not seeing this particular kind of china for the first time.

The Conde, however, took her to another part of the room where he pointed out some examples of rare Meissen and some very early Bow and Chelsea figures.

'Our porcelain was everywhere,' she commented with pride. 'It was in very great demand in the eighteenth century.'

The Conde's grey eyes surveyed her for a second, and she was sure they held a trace of mockery within their depths.

'At that time the English were in the ascendancy with much more than china. This was the age of Sheraton and Hepplewhite. It was a short-lived stardom, though,' he added in that smoothly foreign voice. 'Injudicious planning brought about your downfall.'

Her chin shot up; she forgot for the moment his exalted position, and her own lowly one. They were equals and she was not allowing him to make disparaging comment on her country.

'We still produce beautiful goods,' she stated emphatically. 'Our porcelain manufacturers still export their products to all the important countries of the world!'

'I would not argue the point, *senhorita*, but I still maintain that you've failed to hold your position—the unique and most enviable position which your country held two hundred years ago.' He paused; she said nothing and after a moment he said, in a slightly less smooth and austere manner, 'May I say, *senhorita*, that I admire your loyalty to your country.'

She flushed, aware of being strangely affected by the change in his voice.

'Thank you, Dom Duarte,' she returned shyly. 'It is kind of you to say so.'

Long after she was in her bedroom she was thinking about the evening. It had in many ways been unreal and there were some things that even now had become vague in her mind. But one thing that was not vague was the inescapable magnetism of the Conde. In what way that magnetism affected her she could not tell; all she knew was that his handsome face and arresting personality would be with her for a long while after she had left the lovely coral island of Torassa.

CHAPTER THREE

FOR the following two days Laura was conducted to various parts of the island by Teresa who, every now and then, would become exceedingly expansive, giving Laura details of the island and the people and especially of the Conde himself. But then she would suddenly realise she was saying far too much and immediately change the subject, talking affably about what was in view at that particular time.

'The tide is low and you can see the fringing reef,' she pointed out when they were strolling along the shore, having spent the whole of the morning and part of the afternoon in the rain forest. They had come back tired but both willing to take a stroll along the white sands, watching the little fishing boats and the larger pleasure craft belonging to the more wealthy people of the island. Teresa had already pointed out Dom Duarte's large and graceful yacht, anchored alongside a jetty at the place where his grounds met the palm-fringed beach.

'Beyond the fringing reef there's a barrier reef?'

'Yes,' answered Teresa, 'that's right. The lagoon's in between the two. It's marvellous, swimming in the lagoon; the water's so beautifully calm—and warm, of course.'

Laura nodded.

'It must be warm for coral to live in it.'

The girl looked swiftly at her.

'You know about coral, then?'

'I know a little, yes. I learned at school about reefs,

41

and that they are built up of coral—and other polyps, of course. I know that the temperature of sea water must be sixty-eight degrees fahrenheit for coral to be able to live in it.'

'Look at the lagoon!' said Teresa, changing the subject. 'Doesn't it remind you of something out of a book of fairy tales?'

Laura smiled.

'Or a glossy travel brochure.'

'I expect it does,' mused Teresa, adding after a moment, 'There are no travel brochures giving details of Torassa.'

'Dom Duarte told me that he does not allow tourists on the island.'

'We do have visitors, though. We shall soon have company at the Palacio.'

'You will?' curiously as Laura sensed it was to be one of those times when Teresa would become expansive. Already Laura had learned that Dom Duarte had two sisters and two brothers, all living in Portugal. She also knew about a Portuguese girl called Dona Eduarda de Manso who, it was at one time thought, would become the wife of Dom Duarte. But she had married someone else and was now a widow. She visited the Conde two or three times a year and gossip had it that Dona Eduarda, unhappily married the first time, would eventually marry her first love.

'Yes,' answered Teresa, 'we are to have visitors. One of the sisters of Dom Duarte, Dona Maria Mondego, who lives with her husband in Lisbon, has asked Dom Duarte if he will have her little girl for three months, because her husband has to go abroad and she wants to go with him.'

'And Dom Duarte has agreed to have the little girl?'

'I can understand your surprise, *senhorita*,' returned

Teresa with a grimace, 'because he doesn't appear to be a man who would be interested in children. But he's very kind, really, and he was very sympathetic when Dona Maria said she did not want to be parted from her husband for three months. The little girl, Clara, has her nanny with her, so she'll be quite happy.'

So the nanny was coming to Torassa. Laura could not help feeling envious of this unknown Portuguese girl who was to spend three months on the island.

'When will these two be arriving?' she asked.

'Tomorrow, I think.'

'So soon. I shall meet them, then?'

Teresa nodded. She had been curious about Laura, but had not so much as asked one question as to why she was not remaining at the Palacio. Her fiancé would have told her what little he knew, but that was not very much at all. Laura was most impressed by the girl's reserve, and liked her all the more for it.

'Yes, you'll meet them. The little girl's been here many times, with her parents, so she's used to the Palacio, and to her Uncle Duarte.'

'The nanny ... is she young?'

'About your age, *senhorita*.'

'What's her name?'

'Marianna. It's pretty, isn't it?'

'Very,' smiled Laura, then inquired the age of the child.

'She's five. Marianna has recently begun to teach her. You see, Marianna is a qualified teacher, which is the reason she was engaged by Clara's parents. They do not want her to go to school for several years yet.'

That evening the Conde himself mentioned his visitors.

'They'll be arriving tomorrow afternoon,' he said with his customary aloof detachment. 'I might, I'm afraid, have to take Teresa from you now and then. My young niece can be rather a handful and her nanny becomes a little harassed and tired. If this does happen I shall give Marianna a rest and hand over my niece to Teresa, with whom she gets on very well indeed.'

It was with some astonishment that Laura looked at him, for his words were a revelation. She would never have believed he would trouble himself about the state of mind of a mere servant, especially as that servant was not one of his own.

He and Laura were again in the Blue Lounge; Gigo had served coffee and Dom Duarte poured it out. Although feeling a little ill at ease in his august company, Laura was yet determined to appear cool and confident, since she strongly suspected that the noble Conde would have little or no patience with those who could not command their feelings and behaviour.

'Teresa did mention that your niece and her nanny were paying a visit,' she said, picking up her coffee and meeting those grey eyes over the rim of the cup. 'I expect your niece keeps you alive on these visits.'

Dom Duarte nodded, but absently.

'She's a most attractive child. But, as I've implied, full of mischief.'

'She has no brothers or sisters?'

'Unfortunately no. My sister and her husband had hoped there would be another within two years at the most——' He shrugged his aristocratic shoulders. 'These are the things over which we have no control.'

'Does the little girl have playmates—at home, I mean?'

'Several. But in any case, she would never be a lonely child; she has too much interest in things around her.' Faintly he smiled, and Laura was impressed by the change which even this slight curve of the lips could bring about. Dom Duarte was inordinately handsome even when austere; when he smiled he became devastatingly attractive, and Laura would not have been a woman had she not been affected by this attraction. She considered that the girl he married would be the envy of every friend she had. Laura began to wonder about his parents, sure that they, too, must have been remarkably good-looking.

'She sounds a most interesting child,' mused Laura, putting down her cup. 'I myself am very fond of children, so perhaps, if her nanny does become tired . . .' She allowed her voice to trail off to silence, aware that she had almost taken a liberty. However, to her surprise the Conde, who knew what she had been about to say, told her graciously that he would remember her offer, and perhaps take her up on it.

'Of course,' he went on thoughtfully, 'you won't be here much longer, so there might not be an opportunity of your taking over Clara for a day or so.'

Laura was soon saying goodnight to him; she went out into the garden and wondered what he himself did in the evenings. But a short while later, as she was passing a window at the side of the Palacio, she heard the strains of Beethoven's Fifth Symphony and realised that he was listening to gramophone records.

The gardens were glowing with colour, subdued in parts, but bright in others, as those playing on the fountain. Gold, peach and a delicate green, these were the colours of the hidden lamps which shone on to the fountain and the cascade at the side of the pool. Several terraces lay before Laura as she wandered away from the pool. On one of these was a wide lawn with mature trees dotted here and there, and flower borders intruding subtly into its edges, so that scarcely any of them were straight. Ornamental gardens and parterres occupied the second terrace, and on the third terrace were beautifully fashioned yew and box trees forming peacocks, a heron in flight and many other birds.

The following morning Laura went up to the Gallery to admire the pictures. She had already been there, on more than one occasion, but this time she studied the paintings more carefully, and with the experienced eye of the connoisseur. She saw the flaws, result of damp, she thought, and was in no doubt at all that she could restore these beautiful works of art to their original beauty. On sudden impulse she went back to her room for a notebook in which she then wrote down all that she thought needed to be done. It was an absorbing task and a most interesting one, so it was not at all surprising that she remained unaware of the quiet footsteps treading the carpet behind her. It was the appearance of the man himself, at her side, that made her give a start and drop the notebook in which she had been writing so busily.

Without losing one degree of dignity the Conde stooped and retrieved the notebook. He handed it to her and said, in that suave and foreign voice which was now so familiar to her,

'It would appear that you have been assessing the damage to my pictures?'

She nodded, a trifle flushed and uncomfortable but enthusiastic for all that.

'I could put them right,' was her eager and impulsive assertion. 'I once helped my father with some paintings which had been even more seriously affected by damp than these.' Her smile brought that limpidity to her shy, grey-green eyes and for a fleeting moment the Conde's entire attention was caught.

'What makes you so sure that the damage has been

46

brought about by damp?' he inquired smoothly at length.

'They look exactly as those others I have mentioned.'

'You certainly sound as if you've had experience.' His admission was rather in the sense of a grudging one. Laura tilted her chin unconsciously and told him that she had had a *great deal* of experience.

'If you would allow me to tackle one,' she ventured in a more meek and persuasive tone of voice, 'I would then at least have an opportunity of proving my capabilities in this particular field of art.'

He held out his hand for the notebook, which she immediately passed to him, her heart skipping a beat as the possibility of a prolonged stay at the Palacio loomed clearly on the horizon. She watched him as he opened her book, automatically wishing she had been neater with her writing. Scribbling down information for her own eyes was one thing; that the Conde should want to see those notes was something very different. She noticed the taut profile, unmoving as a statue, and she wondered if he had ever been stirred by any form of emotion. Certainly, she thought, he would never be seen in a temper. But why resort to anger anyway ... when by a mere look from those steely eyes would be censure enough?

He seemed engrossed, and Laura moved away, to stand and stare at another lovely painting. The window was open at the end of the gallery and through it drifted the heady perfume of some tropical flower growing in the gardens below. She thought of the smells from the trading estate where she worked, and sent up a little prayer that the Conde would allow her to try out her skills on at least one of his pictures. To stay here, on this lovely tropical island, would be the most wonderful experience of her life, and one for

47

which she would be forever grateful to the man who made it possible.

Laura turned her head when he moved, and a smile came hesitantly to her lips and hovered there. Her eyes were wide, imploring in a way that was lost on Laura herself but which did not escape the noble lord of Torassa in whose hands her immediate future lay.

'I'll keep this if I may?' A request that was really a firm statement, and Laura's smile deepened. It did not for one single moment enter his head that she might refuse to let him take it away. Not that she wanted to do so—on the contrary, she was very keen that he should read what she had written, scribbly though her writing was.

'Certainly, sir.' The last word came out unconsciously; the Conde looked down at her from his incredible height and said with a trace of cold hauteur,

'I prefer that you address me as Dom Duarte, *senhorita*.'

She bit her lip, nodding meekly.

'Yes—I understand,' she said, noticing that he had put her little book into the pocket of his white linen jacket.

'There will be another visitor arriving this afternoon,' he said after a slight pause. 'My friend, Dona Eduarda de Manso, so there will be three of us for dinner.' Without another word he turned on his heel and strode along the length of the gallery, his lithe body swinging with a noble gait, his dark head erect upon broad arrogant shoulders.

What a man! More like a king, thought Laura, her mind switching to the image which she and Avice had conjured up of the lord of Torassa. What a lot she would have to tell Avice when she saw her next week—Next week?

'I'll keep my fingers crossed that he'll like what he reads!' she exclaimed in a whisper as she followed the path just taken by the Conde. 'Oh, but it'll be heaven to stay here for a little while!' And what satisfaction she would derive from restoring one of the paintings. If she were given the chance, and was successful in pleasing the Conde, then of course he would seriously consider allowing her to set to work on the others, with the result that she would be here for the six months—or perhaps longer.

The two figures down on the patio were indistinct, but Laura knew who they were. She had met Dona Eduarda at the same time as she had met Marianna and Clara, all of them having flown in on the same aeroplane, which was going on to the island of Sri Lanka. Marianna was youthful, of a happy disposition and yet serious-minded and studious. So quiet, too, as if aware of her place as a servant. She managed the child very well indeed, but it was easy to see that there were times when she had her difficulties, for even after only an hour or so in her company, Laura had taken in the fact that the child could be a handful. She had a strong will, which itself bred obstinacy. Dona Eduarda had been in Laura's company only a few minutes but, in some strange indefinable way, the two women took an instant dislike to one another. And yet, despite her own dislike for the Portuguese girl, Laura had to admit that she would make an admirable wife for the illustrious owner of the Palacio de Mauredo, being able to manage the numerous servants that were necessary in so massive an establishment. Dona Eduarda was tall and slender, with black hair and glittering eyes that were as arrogant as those of her friend the Conde. Her voice too was unusual, having a vibrating coldness about it that

49

was totally without depth. Laura had the swift impression that worldly possessions were all that the girl was interested in. And in fact Laura was later to learn that her first marriage had made Dona Eduarda into a millionairess, her husband having left her everything he owned.

The two figures down there on the patio moved into the light and were then easily discernible. Dona Eduarda was attired in a slinky black dress and on both wrists the diamonds glittered like stars. Dom Duarte was in a dinner jacket and even from here the contrast of white shirt against the bronzed skin of his neck and face was·startling. At last Laura turned and went from the balcony into her bedroom, walking slowly towards the long gilt-framed mirror, where she stood critically to examine the reflection that looked back at her. Of only medium height, she had neither the self-assurance nor the cool confidence of the Portuguese girl. Height did make a difference, Laura decided, thinking of the Conde, and what his height did for him. She looked at her hair, a shining mass of russet-brown dropping to her shoulders. She had altered the style slightly and now the ends turned under in a pageboy bob. Her eyes ... Like her mother's, her father had always said, large and beautiful and tender. Her mouth, generous but not large. Dona Eduarda's mouth was wide and inviting and faintly sensuous, like the Conde's. Despite the strong veneer of coldness that encompassed both Dom Duarte and his glamorous friend, Laura was in no doubt at all that they could display an inordinate passion in their lovemaking—Laura checked her thoughts with a swiftness born of embarrassment. She found she was actually blushing at her own mind-wanderings.

And yet she could not check these visions of those two locked in a passionate embrace. She had noticed

Dom Duarte's hands, slender and perfectly-formed with the skin drawn tight and the nails immaculate. They were sensitive, yet she knew they had a hidden strength that could hurt if need be. And now she could imagine those attractive hands touching Dona Eduarda's cheek, her neck, her firm mature curves ...

With a frown and a shake of her head Laura turned from the mirror, sprayed her hair with perfume, then went from the room, her feelings very mixed as she imagined her own position at the dinner table. Surely the two would have preferred being together? Yet Dom Duarte had not given any indication that he would prefer Laura to dine elsewhere than in the lovely high-ceilinged saloon where a footman was ready to serve his master and his guests. In fact, Dom Duarte had said, in the Gallery that morning, that there would be three of them at the dinner table that evening.

Oh, well, the evening would pass, thought Laura; and it might be interesting to watch the two together and attempt to ascertain whether or not there was any real basis for the rumours of which Teresa had spoken.

They were in the lounge when Laura entered and the Conde rose at once, inviting her to sit down. He poured her a drink and she thanked him, profoundly aware of a pair of very dark eyes fixed upon her—Dona Eduarda's eyes. The girl spoke, with the merest trace of an accent.

'I hear that you came to do some work on Dom Duarte's paintings?' The cold voice was dispassionate, arrogant. 'Your father should have come, but he died. I'm sorry to hear that.'

Laura looked directly at her, fully aware that the girl spoke automatically, saying what she knew she ought to say and not what she really meant. Laura felt a tinge of contempt at the hypocrisy of the girl who, after all, need not have said anything about the death of Laura's father in the first place.

The Conde spoke into the silence, easing it.

'What did you think about my young niece, Miss Conroy? I saw you playing ball with her and Marianna soon after they arrived.'

'I think she's a very charming child,' answered Laura sincerely. 'And so attractive in looks.'

'Pretty, yes.' His eyes surveyed her before resting on Dona Eduarda's face. Laura, wondering if he were comparing them, glanced down at her dress, a white cotton one with a pleated skirt and tight-fitting bodice. She had made it herself and until now had liked it very much, feeling proud of her achievement as a dress-maker. Now, she felt a dowd, and wanted to make her exit from the presence of these two polished aristocrats whose attire was superlatively correct. Dom Duarte certainly appeared to be interested in her dress at this moment, she noticed, and her discomfiture increased. The Portuguese girl was reclining in her chair, casually sipping her drink, her dark eyes moving very slowly from Dom Duarte's face to that of Laura.

'Clara's here for three months, you said?' Dona Eduarda spoke at length, addressing Dom Duarte.

'That's correct. Maria desires to accompany Felipe on his business trip.'

'I do feel that Maria should put Clara before Felipe,' said Dona Eduarda with a frown. 'A young child needs her mother around all the time. Why, Clara will have forgotten what Maria looks like long before the three months is up.'

The Conde shot her a strange glance and Laura, with keen perception, guessed what he would have said, had he and Dona Eduarda been alone.

'You believe that a wife should put her husband

second, after her children?' Aloud he merely said that he could understand Maria's desire to be with Felipe, and that as Clara was five years old she could not possibly forget what her mother looked like. Soon after that they went in to dinner; Laura, even more uncomfortable than she had expected to be, was silent for the most part, but now and then Dom Duarte would speak to her, bringing her into the conversation. However, soon the Portuguese girl would intervene with some irrelevant comment which would automatically switch the subject and once again leave Laura out. She was relieved when at last the dinner was over and they all went into the lounge for coffee. With little obvious haste, Laura nevertheless finished hers quickly and, rising, asked to be excused.

'Certainly,' returned Dom Duarte in his clipped and alien voice.

'Goodnight, Miss Conroy,' said Dona Eduarda. And then she added, 'You are not going to bed yet, though?' Her eyes flickered to the French clock on the mantelpiece.

'No, I usually take a stroll in the garden first.'

'You do?' in a strange tone, and her eyes now went to the Conde. 'A habit of yours, Duarte. Do you ever meet out there?'

Laura went hot, while the Conde's brow creased in a darkling frown. But he merely looked at Laura, who had managed to reach the door without appearing in too much of a hurry to leave the room.

Goodnight, *senhorita*. Don't go too far from the Palacio; I think we shall have rain before very long.'

She went out, closing the door softly behind her. A strange and inexplicable heaviness had settled on her; she knew that this evening's meal was not nearly so pleasant an experience as those that had gone before, but what really puzzled her was why she should be feeling so dejected about it.

The following morning she awoke to the song of birds in the sunshine and, throwing open the drapes, she stepped out on to the balcony. Lovely! Sun-drenched island with tall palms and white sandy beaches! The mountains stood towards the east, lush and soft beneath the tropical sky. In the opposite direction was the infinite expanse of the Indian Ocean, aquamarine and scarcely moving. On the horizon a ship seemed to be immobile, while closer to the shore, just beyond the lagoon, a yacht could be seen, its white and red sails outlined against the brilliant blue of the sky. It was not the vessel Teresa had pointed out as belonging to the Conde.

Laura went in and bathed, then put on a bikini. A robe was snatched and within less than thirty seconds she was hurrying across the grounds of the Palacio towards a tree-fringed path which led on to the Conde's private beach. She was not by any means a strong swimmer, but she could manage a few strokes, and these brought her close to the reef. She turned on her back and floated, staring up at the sky. She felt as though she were in a dream, with the reality of the world a million miles away. The high-rise flats which she saw from her window at home seemed to have no substance; they had melted into nothingness because here, in this tropical paradise, nature reigned supreme, undespoiled by the avid desire of man to destroy.

A sound reached her ears and she realised she was not alone, but the sound set her every nerve alert. A child's scream followed it immediately and she turned, to stare with rising terror at the small figure in the water, some distance from where she was.

Clara! What on earth was the child doing here—?

54

But there was no time for asking questions! Laura began to swim towards the child, her fear a blockage in her throat. For she knew she would have difficulty in swimming out that far—and what about getting back to the shore?

'I c-can't do it!' she cried, even while she was endeavouring to put more strength into her strokes.

Another scream rang out, but at least the child was managing to keep herself afloat.

'I'm coming, Clara!' Laura tried to make her voice sound loud, so that it would reach the child, but she was so breathless already that she wondered if it carried at all. But at last she was with the child, holding her even though she was struggling.

'Don't, dear. Please don't struggle.' Laura's strength was at a low ebb, and her breathing was giving her some trouble. And then, just as she felt she and the little girl would drown together, here, so close to the shore, she heard a call and managed a little gasp of thankfulness as she saw Dona Eduarda swimming strongly towards them.

'Thank God!' A great sob escaped her as she turned. But she remembered no more, for her head had hit the ragged jutting rock that was part of the reef and that, along with the utter fatigue assailing her whole body, robbed her of consciousness.

CHAPTER FOUR

SHE came to a few moments later, aware that she was being carried along the shore, carried as if she were no heavier than the child she had tried to rescue.

'Clara!' she cried. 'Is she——?'

'Quite safe.' The voice was ice against Laura's ear. 'Dona Eduarda fetched her out. It was most fortunate that she happened to be on hand.'

'Yes.' Laura, dazed though she still was, could not possibly miss the hostility contained in the Conde's voice. 'You—you must have been on—on hand, too.'

'I happened to look through my window,' he returned, 'but Dona Eduarda had my niece safe by this time.'

'Oh ... well, thank you for saving me.' Laura felt a spasm of pain in her head and turned, resting it against him. His chest was bare; she was gradually having it borne in upon her clouded mind that he had probably only just got out of bed when he looked through that window. 'How did Clara come to be in the water?' she managed to ask presently.

The Conde stiffened.

'That,' he replied with an undertone of wrath, 'is a question which I am intending to ask you.'

'Me ...?' She sighed, aware that consciousness was about to leave her again. She did not, therefore, remember being brought into the house, or being taken up to her bedroom. But she regained consciousness just as Dom Duarte was putting her on to the bed. She felt his warm hands on her near-naked body, felt him above her as he bent to examine the cut on her head. She knew that someone else had followed him into the room and as he moved she saw Teresa, her big brown eyes anxious and yet faintly accusing.

'I'll have the doctor here shortly.' Laura heard the Conde's words and wondered why his voice was harsh. 'Meanwhile, see to her; don't let that wound bleed if you can help it.'

'No, Dom Duarte, I will see to it, as you say.'

Laura opened her mouth to speak, then decided against it. She had no idea why, but she was aware of some strange warning, aware that all was not as— within her mind—it appeared.

'You're badly hurt, Miss Conroy.' Teresa's concern was genuine but in her tone was censure. 'You heard Dom Duarte say that the doctor would be here soon?'

'Yes,' was Laura's brief reply.

'I'll put a thick pad of cotton wool on it. But first, you must get out of your bikini and put on a night-gown.'

This was fetched and a few minutes later Laura was between the sheets.

'I'll just go for the cotton wool.' Teresa went from the room, returning presently with a bowl of warm water and a roll of cotton wool. The wound, deep and very painful, was bathed and then the pad applied.

'If you can hold it in place, *senhorita*?'

'Yes.' Laura held it against her temple. She waited for the girl to speak, seeing her hesitancy but sure she would speak eventually.

'*Senhorita*, the Conde is very angry, I fear.'

'Yes?' said Laura again, still disinclined to talk about what had happened out there, by the reef.

'Clara ... you should not have enticed her into the sea.'

57

'Enticed?' frowned Laura.

'She has told her uncle all about it.'

'I see.' Even though her thoughts were by no means as clear as usual, Laura was beginning to see a glimmer of light. 'What did Clara tell her uncle?'

'Of how she was in the garden and you persuaded her to go into the sea with you. Of course, Clara can swim, and I suppose, *senhorita*, that you thought it would be all right. But Marianna is here to look after her, and she was in a panic when she discovered the little girl's absence from her bed.'

'From her bed?' repeated Laura. 'You said she was in the garden.'

'That's right. She had been very naughty to leave her bed in any case. It is the first time she has done such a thing, so Marianna tells me.'

'And Clara told her uncle that I persuaded her to come with me for a bathe?' It was clear to Laura that the child had told this lie in order to escape the anger of the Conde.

'Yes. She told him as soon as you and she were safely on the beach. I expect her uncle questioned her immediately.'

Laura was left to digest all this, for Teresa went from the room, saying she would be back shortly.

What must she do? The idea of the Conde's believing that she could have taken it upon herself to persuade his niece to forget the authority of her nanny was so troubling that Laura's first reaction was to disillusion Dom Duarte as soon as possible. But swiftly on this decision came the position of the child in all this. Clara had done wrong, apparently, by leaving her bedroom in the first place. But having escaped the surveillance of her nanny she went still further, taking advantage of her freedom by deciding to go for a swim. How she had

58

got into difficulties was not important. What was important was the little girl's peace of mind. True, she had told a lie in order to escape the punishment which her austere uncle would most assuredly have inflicted, but to Laura, who both liked and understood children, the lie was in no way wicked. It was impulsive, Laura was sure, told on the spur of the moment when Clara was questioned by her uncle. Laura thought, too, that Clara would not be herself in any case, not after the frightening experience she had just been through.

A sigh escaped Laura as she recalled her high hopes of being allowed to work on at least one of Dom Duarte's pictures. Now she would be packed off home on the next plane, the Conde considering her to be a potential danger to the safety of his niece. Well, that was that. Laura felt she could not give the child away, not even for the prospect of staying on the island.

The doctor arrived and frowned darkly as he examined the wound. Dom Duarte was not present, but Teresa later told Laura that she could not be moved while the injury was so bad.

'The doctor was troubled, and he told Dom Duarte that you cannot possibly go home yet awhile.'

Laura, automatically putting a hand to her heavily-bandaged head, asked Teresa if she had any idea at all just how long it would be before she could leave Torassa.

'Did the doctor give Dom Duarte any indication at all?' she added.

Teresa shook her head.

'No, but the Conde is coming in to see you shortly, so you will be able to talk to him.' Teresa's voice carried anxiety; she liked Laura and it was plain that she was not happy at the idea of the telling off which Laura was about to receive. On impulse Laura said,

'Don't worry about me, Teresa. I shall not be too put out by the Conde's anger.'

'Well ... He can be very cutting, *senhorita*.'

'I don't doubt that for one moment. However, a dressing-down doesn't last too long. In any case, I don't expect Dom Duarte will want to remain long with me.'

'No, that is something. He and Dona Eduarda are going out to lunch with some friends of his.'

He entered the room about ten minutes later and his abrupt inclination of the head was an order for Teresa to leave, which she did, but she glanced commiseratingly at the patient as she passed her on the way to the door.

'The doctor tells me that you will have to remain here for some time.' The crisp foreign voice held little or no anxiety and Laura knew a strange and inexplicable little pang that the Conde was not in the least concerned about her condition. Even though he was angry, he could have shown a little sympathy, she thought. But looking into that forbidding face she could think of him only as a feudal lord about to censure one of his vassals.

'So Teresa says,' returned Laura in her quiet, serious voice.

'I have come to seek an explanation of your incredible conduct in persuading my niece to go into the sea with you.'

Laura swallowed hard; she was not clever at telling untruths and it took her some time to think out what she must say. Her long pause served only to convince the Conde of her guilt.

'I really don't have any explanation to offer,' said Laura at last, deliberately injecting a note of apology into her voice. 'It was very wrong of me.'

'You must have known that Marianna is in complete charge of Clara?'

'Yes, of course.'

The Conde was frowning darkly.

'Having enticed Clara into the sea, why did you then let her get into difficulties?'

'I—er—thought she was a stronger swimmer than she turned out to be.' No use trying to prevaricate in any way, or to defend herself. Any slip on her part would be instantly noticed by a man with the keen perception of the Conde, and Laura strongly suspected that she would be in even more trouble should he discover that she herself had lied to him in order to cover up for his niece.

His eyes were wide with wrathful astonishment at her giving him an answer that was so weak.

'You mean to say that you took it for granted that a child of five could swim that far out and get back to the shore?' A muscle moved at the side of his mouth, betraying anger determinedly suppressed. But his gaze was icily scathing, his whole manner one of censure not unmingled with contempt. 'What kind of a woman are you to lie there so calmly and tell me this?'

'I'm very sorry,' was all she could find to say. Misery edged her voice, but obviously the Conde had no intention other than to subject her to a scathing reprimand, and this he did, her misery being ignored. She was hot by the time he had finished what he had to say and it was with some difficulty that she repressed a sudden urge to let him have the truth.

'It wasn't as if you did anything to save her——' The Conde broke off and Laura saw that his emotion had caused this. He was seeing his niece drowned ...

Laura stared into his face and said uncomprehendingly,

'I didn't try to save her? I don't know how you can say a thing like that, Dom Duarte. I was——'

'You were swimming away from her when Dona Eduarda saw you. She was horrified at your intention to leave my niece to drown——' Again he broke off and Laura noticed that tiny beads of perspiration were standing out on his forehead.

So Dona Eduarda had lied too? Laura, her head throbbing madly with the pain from the wound, suddenly did not care about anything except getting back home to her little flat. It *was* home, after all, a place that she herself had made, and it offered peace and comfort that had now taken on enormous proportions. To be back, away from these foreign people who told unnecessary lies, spiteful lies.

Clara she could forgive, and indeed she did forgive her; Dona Eduarda she could neither forgive nor understand. For what reason had she lied? Laura shrugged off the question, giving a deep sigh.

'How long must I stay here?' she asked, not troubling to put respect into her voice. 'I naturally have no wish to continue being a trouble to you.'

She heard him draw a wrathful breath. But his manner and tone were coldly dispassionate as he said,

'The doctor must decide. He will say when you are fit to travel.'

She felt the tears behind her eyes.

'I hope it won't be long,' she said distractedly. 'I want to go away from here.'

The Conde rose majestically and left the room; Teresa came in and asked Laura if she wanted anything to eat.

'No, thank you, Teresa.'

The girl stood by the bed, her underlip caught in her teeth.

'You've had no breakfast, *senhorita*.'

'I don't want anything at all.' Laura looked at her, noticing the compassion on her face. So soft and gentle a face. No wonder everyone liked her. 'It's good of you to be concerned, Teresa, but there isn't anything you can do.'

The girl hesitated and then,

'You are not the kind of person, *senhorita*, to entice a little girl out into the sea. And most certainly you're not the one to swim away and leave anyone to drown.'

'But I did those things,' returned Laura, the pain in her head so excruciating now that she felt she could cry out in agony.

'If you say so.' Teresa's voice was very quiet; her eyes were questioning. 'I cannot accuse you of telling untruths, can I?'

Laura managed to say, in spite of the pain filling her mind,

'You believed at first that I had done those things.'

The girl nodded, but weakly.

'Clara and Dona Eduarda had spoken, and I heard what they said because I was there when Dom Duarte and Dona Eduarda were mentioning it. Perhaps I did believe it,' she added doubtfully, 'but perhaps I did not.'

So she had one friend in this great Palacio, thought Laura, and it was amazing just what comfort the knowledge gave her.

'It's kind of you to believe in me, Teresa, but I will ask you to keep your opinions entirely to yourself—not mentioning them even to your fiancé. Will you promise me this?'

The girl's eyes were perceptive.

'I think I see,' she said after a thoughtful pause. 'I will do as you ask, *senhorita*.'

'Thank you.'

'And now—will you in turn do something for me?'

'If it is possible—yes, of course I will.'

'Have something to eat.' It was almost a plea, and Laura felt it would be churlish to refuse when the girl was so very anxious about her. She managed a smile and said yes, she would have some toast and a cup of coffee.

Two days passed, days of sheer boredom for Laura, as the Conde would not let Teresa stay with her at all. She was given a few English magazines and nothing else. It was plain that the Conde had no time for her, believing as he did that she had enticed Clara out into the sea and then intended abandoning her. Laura's notebook was returned to her one mealtime, Teresa bringing it in on the tray. On the third day the doctor said she could get up the following afternoon for a few hours. He had called every day and Laura was acutely conscious of the trouble and expense to which she was putting the Conde.

She now admitted that it had been sheer folly to have come in the first place and, looking back, she could scarcely believe that she could have been so impulsive as to have even contemplated coming out to Torassa. Well, what was done was done and the sooner she could leave the better it would suit her.

'The pain is still bad?' The doctor asked the question after having taken a look at the injury. When Laura said it was becoming more bearable he said he would give her some tablets which would ease it altogether. 'These others were not strong, but I had to be cautious. One has to be with drugs.'

She felt amazingly weak when, the following afternoon, she got up and sat on the balcony, on the comfortable chair which Teresa had procured for her. The sun was warm, the perfumes from the garden sweet and delicate on the air. Birds with bright plumage flew from one tree to another, their song a delight to the ears. Clara, playing hide and seek with Marianna, glanced upwards as she ran across the lawn, and instantly looked away again. Laura, more herself now, felt she must have a word or two with that young lady before she left the Palacio. Forgiveness was all right in its way, but a scolding would not come amiss.

'Are you comfortable?' asked Teresa, coming on to the balcony with a tray on which there was a glass of milk and some biscuits.

'Very. But I don't think I shall be here long,' added Laura with a grimace.

'You feel weak?' The girl's voice, with its trace of an accent, was gentle and anxious. 'You lost a great deal of blood, you know.'

'Yes, I believe so.' Laura looked at the tray, which Teresa had placed on the table. 'Thank you for the refreshments,' she said with a smile.

'I believe that Dom Duarte will be in to speak to you later this afternoon.'

'Oh ...' Nerves fluttered slightly. 'Have you any idea what he wants to say to me?'

'I think,' answered Teresa guardedly, 'that it's about your departure.'

Laura nodded absently. There was nothing else which the Conde would want to see her about.

He came up after she had got back into bed. Dressed casually in a polo-necked white cotton shirt and brown linen slacks, he appeared a little less austere than she had remembered him. His grey eyes flickered over her face, then down to her hands where they rested on the coverlet.

'Teresa tells me that you feel weak?' Dispassionate tones that might have been for a total stranger. 'It's probably because you've been lying in bed.'

'Yes, I expect it is.' She drew a deep breath. 'Dom Duarte, I am very sorry indeed for all this trouble I'm causing you. I feel exceedingly blameworthy for coming to Torassa. It was stupidly impulsive of me.'

'It's a pity, *senhorita*, that you didn't think a little more about it in the first place.'

She nodded unhappily.

'I agree. But everyone commits an impulsive act some time in their lives.'

Dom Duarte's straight black brows had shot up even before she had finished speaking.

'Are you making excuses for your precipitate action in coming here, believing as you did that I would condone your deceit?'

She drew a breath, fervently wishing she were not under such an obligation to him, for nothing would have given her more satisfaction than to forget her tranquil disposition for a space and give him a piece of her mind. He was too arrogant by far, too superior and full of his own importance. A good set-down would perhaps bring him from his lofty pedestal! However, she *was* under an obligation to him, so she prudently controlled her impulses.

'I'm not making excuses,' she said, looking at him from where she rested against the white embroidered pillows. 'But I am trying to say that no one is infallible. It is human to err,' she quoted defensively.

The Conde passed this by unheeded.

'I've been speaking with the doctor, who tells me that you will be fit to travel on the plane which leaves Torassa on Monday next.'

Five days ... They would not pass quickly enough

66

for Laura. She was nodding, and heard herself say,

'I shall make sure I have my strength back by then, Dom Duarte.'

'I hope so,' said the Conde, and left the room.

Laura got up at once, determined to regain the strength that seemed to have left her legs. She dressed and went down to the courtyard, where she found a shady seat beneath the trees. She put a hand to her head and frowned. She had always hated bandages, even small ones. Now her head was swathed in them. She fell into a mood of reflection, thinking about Avice and all she would have to tell her, next week, when she returned to England, and that scene of high-rise flats and smoky chimneys, of bustling people and noisy traffic. A voice came to her after a while and she turned her head. Clara ... Laura said, a hint of sharpness in her voice,

'Why are you alone? Where is your nanny?'

The little girl came forward, her big brown eyes fixed on the bandage.

'I am very sorry,' she said surprisingly, just the trace of a foreign accent in her otherwise perfect English. 'Does your head hurt much now?'

'No, not much. Where is Marianna?'

'Ironing my dress—my party dress, or one of them. I'm going to Isabella's birthday party in a few minutes. My uncle's taking me in his car. Isabella lives in a big house on the cliff.'

'Tell me, Clara,' said Laura sternly, 'why did you tell a lie about how you came to be in the sea?'

Clara's face went a bright pink.

'That's what I really came to you for. I saw you walking to this place and managed to get away from Marianna for a minute or two. She thinks I've gone up to the nursery to fetch my doll. I am very sorry,' she said again.

'No doubt you are, but I would very much like to know more about it. How did you come to be in the sea?'

The child's eyes came alive. It was plain that she was not now troubled about her guilt, but more interested in relating her escapade. Laura listened with interest, learning that Clara, having risen early, donned a swimsuit and went to the shore to collect shells. But then she thought she would like to paddle and went into the water.

'A wave came,' she went on, 'just a little wave, but it made me fall into the water——' Clara laughed then, and Laura saw that this mishap had not troubled the child in the least. 'It was lovely and warm. I could swim and I went out, thinking I would get to the yacht——'

'The yacht!' exclaimed Laura. 'Why, you silly little girl! That yacht was a very long way from the shore!'

'It belongs to Isabella's father,' Clara informed her. 'It did not seem to be far at all.'

'What happened then?'

'I got tired after a while and could not swim. The beach seemed a long way off!' Clara's voice became high-pitched as she relived those moments of fear. 'I thought I would drown—and then you came and held me up.' The child's wide intelligent forehead was creased and her mouth quivered. 'I did not want to tell a lie, but my uncle would have spanked me, and he hurts!' She looked down, clearly ashamed of herself. 'I knew, you see, that he wouldn't spank you, and so—so I told a lie and said I was only in the garden and you said to me, "Come on, Clara, and we'll go for a swim." And I said to my uncle that I knew this was wrong and so I would not go with you. But afterwards I did go with you because you kept on asking me to go with you.' All this time the child had her head averted, and her words became rather jumbled, spoken as they were, under some stress. 'I wish I had not told a lie, *senhorita*, because I like you, and it isn't nice when my uncle talks about you——'

'He talks about me?' The question escaped involuntarily and the child nodded.

'He said to Aunt Eduarda that you were a nuisance in his home, that you English people had no sense of what was the right thing to do ...' Clara tailed off as Laura lifted a hand. 'Don't you want to hear any more?' the child asked.

'No, thank you,' answered Laura tersely. 'I think you had better run along to your nanny; she'll have missed you already.'

Clara seemed to swallow something in her throat.

'You came to mend some pictures, didn't you?'

'I said, run along. It wouldn't do for your uncle to come and find you here, talking to me.'

'I wish you could have stayed to mend the pictures,' went on Clara, uncomfortable but undaunted. 'I looked at the pictures, but I couldn't find one that needed mending. Perhaps Uncle Duarte thinks they are all right as they are?' Clara looked at Laura for enlightenment, but Laura merely shook her head impatiently. The last thing she wanted was for the Conde to appear and curtly tell the child to return to her nanny. 'If the pictures were really needing mending ...' Clara's voice trailed off once more as Laura made a sharp gesture with her hand. 'I'll go,' she said hurriedly and, turning, she sped away and was lost to view among the trees bordering the courtyard.

Laura rose from her seat and stood for a while admiring her immediate surroundings. The floor of the courtyard was a picture in itself, being made up of alternating white and red lozenges, the former made from marble, the latter from jasper. These must have been brought to the island from somewhere else, Torassa itself being a coral island. There was a fountain in the courtyard, with weeping cherry trees close to it, their long branches of blossom trailing the ground. Other trees and bushes flaunted colours from delicate pinks to deepest crimson. High ferns provided a green lacing for the fragile beauty of the passion flowers and the delightful bird of paradise. A statue of white marble stood by the fountain, a torch held in one hand, a torch which was lit at night, giving a deep red glow to the more insipid pink of the morning glory bush.

Laura wandered through the high wide arch and entered the garden. Her legs were still weak, but she was determined to overcome the weakness, and without delay. Nothing must prevent her from leaving Torassa next Monday.

Dona Eduarda was on the lawn, basking in the sunshine, and she glanced up as Laura appeared, her supercilious eyes remaining much longer on the disfiguring bandage than was necessary. It was as if she were deliberately trying to make Laura feel inferior.

Laura was undecided whether or not to walk on, with merely a nod in the girl's direction, but Dona Eduarda spoke, asking Laura how she was feeling now.

'Better, thanks,' she answered abruptly.

'You had a nasty bump. It's to be hoped you're not scarred for life.'

'I don't think so.' Laura had no option but to stop, as the Portuguese girl was speaking again, saying that one never could tell with a gash such as Laura had received.

'It was deep, the doctor said, and so you ought to be prepared to find you've a nasty scar that might never go away.' Dona Eduarda had no reason to be spiteful, Laura told herself reasonably, so why was she being like this?

But why had she lied, saying that Laura had been about to abandon Clara when she was in such distress? Laura had had no intention of questioning the girl, but something over which she had no control resulted in her saying,

'I believe you told Dom Duarte that I was swimming away from Clara when you first saw me?'

Dona Eduarda stared at her unflinchingly and replied,

'I told him what I saw, yes. Is there any reason why I shouldn't have done so?' The voice of arrogance grated on Laura's ears even more than the actual content of the girl's words. What a thoroughly unlikeable person she was! Laura, unused to such people, was more anxious to leave Torassa than ever.

'What you told the Conde was not the truth,' she said accusingly.

'Not——!' Dona Eduarda stared in amazement, her colour rising along with her anger. 'How dare you accuse me of lying? Explain yourself, girl!' She sat upright in her chair, in an attitude of command. 'I want to know just what you are insinuating!'

Pale but resolute, Laura told her that she *had* lied when she said she saw her swimming away.

'You know very well that I was holding Clara up, as best I could. I myself am not a swimmer, merely being able to do a few strokes, but I would never have swum away and left a little child to drown.' The very idea was incredible to Laura's mind. No one with any compassion at all would commit so callous an act.

Dona Eduarda listened without so much as a flicker of an eyelid, her composure totally unimpaired by what Laura had said.

'I'm afraid the bang you received affected your brain, Miss Conroy. In view of this I shall overlook your absurd accusation and not demand an apology from you.' She relaxed, picked up the magazine which was lying on the grass beside her chair and, opening it, she began to read. Flushing hotly, Laura turned on her heel and strode away, back towards the house, and the sanctuary of her bedroom.

CHAPTER FIVE

ALTHOUGH by the Saturday Laura was able to get up at the normal time, and to stay up all day, she was not invited to dine with the Conde and Dona Eduarda. Not that she wanted to; she would most certainly have made some excuse had the Conde profferred an invitation. Nevertheless, she felt slighted, after having dined with the Conde before. She had her evening meal in her room, as she had been doing since the accident, and then she went for a stroll in the grounds of the Palacio, walking amidst the lighted shrubberies and flower beds. It was lonely and still, with the only sound that of the cicadas whirring in the trees. A cooling breeze blew in from the sea, stealing exotic perfumes on the way. Laura wandered on, passing out of the grounds on to the beach where palms, silhouetted against a moonlit sky, waved gently above the soft white sand. She watched fishermen dragging their nets in the placid Indian Ocean, noticed the yacht with its red and white sails and remembered that Clara had said it belonged to her friend's father. One more day to go and then she would be packing her suitcases in readiness for her departure on Monday at midday. Just a few hours left, in fact, to enjoy the peace and tranquillity of this ocean paradise, this coral island which had managed to remain untouched by tourism.

A dark figure looming up from the direction of some rocky caves by the headland caught her attention and she had an impulse to turn and hasten back to the safety of the Palacio gardens. However, she checked the impulse, assuring herself that she could not possibly be in any danger here, where the fishermen were within calling distance. The figure turned out to be a man, strolling leisurely along the shore, as she herself was doing. He said a greeting in Portuguese to which Laura answered,

'Good evening.'

The man stopped and said in perfect English,

'Good evening to you, madam. What part of England do you come from?'

Laura stopped, though reluctantly, her one swift thought being that the Conde would frown darkly upon so casual a meeting as this. The proprieties were strictly observed in Portugal, she knew, so it was reasonable to assume that this would apply with similar rigidity on the island of Torassa. However, it was soon borne in on her that she was leaving the Conde's house very soon, and in any case, it was most unlikely that he would hear of this meeting with a stranger. She noticed the man's eyes settle on her bandage and wondered what he was thinking.

'I come from Birmingham,' she answered, examining his face in the moonlight. It was clear-skinned, with high cheekbones and an unlined forehead from which the hair was prematurely receding—for she guessed his age to be no more than twenty-five at the most.

'From Birmingham? You haven't an accent,' he added with a laugh.

Laura liked him, liked the frank eyes, the wide and generous mouth, the spontaneous way he had laughed.

'What part of England do you come from?' she asked.

'Liverpool.'

'Well, you haven't an accent, either.'

'So I'm told.' He paused a moment, undecided, and then, 'You've hurt yourself?'

'I did it in the sea—caught my head on a rough piece of coral.'

'The reef? It can be dangerous.' Another hesitant moment ensued before he said, 'Do you live here, or are you just a visitor, like me?'

'I'm a visitor.'

'You noticed I didn't ask if you were a tourist?' he said in some amusement. 'The lordly Conde Duarte André Volante de Taviro Mauredo of Torassa guards his domain jealously from the despoliation wrought by the modern traveller.'

'I don't blame him.'

'Nor do I. My sister lives here, you see—married to one of the island's nobility.'

'She is?' Laura returned with interest.

'Yes; his name is Senhor Pedro de Salzadaz. They live in the big house at the end of the shore——' He pointed and Laura nodded.

'It's a lovely house. I've been past it several times when I've taken a stroll along that way.'

'Where are you staying?'

There was a moment's hesitation before she answered with a laugh,

'At the Palacio de Mauredo.'

'At——!' The young man stared in disbelief. 'How come?'

She gave another laugh.

'You're not very flattering,' she told him, at the same time marvelling at the easy way in which they had drifted into conversation. 'However, I suppose I *am* out of my element at that magnificent palace.' She went on to explain how she came to be here, omitting nothing except the incident in the sea and the untruths told by Clara and Don Eduarda.

'So you've to go back on Monday, you say? That's tough luck.'

'I'm not sorry, really,' she rejoined with truth. 'It's all a bit overpowering, I'm afraid.'

'Not used to their way of life, eh? I myself was a little lost on my first visit, but Pedro's all right. I imagine, though, that the Conde's just about as stiff as they come?'

'Very austere and formal, yes, he is,' she replied musingly. 'Very handsome, though,' she added.

'I know. I've seen him. Pedro and Melanie are visitors to his house, but they've never had an invitation that arrived while I've been here.'

'You'd like to visit the Palacio?'

'Rather! It must be a treasure house of antiques?'

'It is, indeed.'

'Look, we haven't introduced ourselves. My name's Rex. What's yours?' Laura told him and he said, 'How about a little supper in that café in town?'

'I've had a meal, but thank you all the same.' She spoke against her inclination, as it would have been nice to visit the café with a companion. She had been there on her own, just for coffee, but knew that at night it was a gay, well-lighted place where a band of musicians played folk music while people dined on local food and wine.

'So have I, as a matter of fact. Well, perhaps we could just go to the café for a drink of wine and a snack?'

The prospect was certainly attractive and Laura soon found herself saying,

'Yes, all right.'

'It'll take us twenty minutes or so to get there——' Rex looked at the bandage. 'Do you feel up to a walk of that length?'

'Of course. I love walking.'

'Your injury's well on the mend, then?' he said, falling into step beside her as she began to retrace her own steps along the beach.

'Yes, I did it over a week ago.'

'I'm sorry you're leaving on Monday,' Rex was saying over half an hour later when he and Laura were seated in a secluded corner of the café, a bottle of wine on the table, and a dish of salad and various meats. They each had a long fork, with which they now and then took up some of the salad or piece of meat. The lights were very low, and on every table a candle shone from a tall red tumbler. It was a romantic place to be, with the music from the main café quietly drifting to this rather remote corner which was sheltered by palms in gleaming brass urns.

'How long will you be here?' Laura's gaze was pensive as she watched Rex pour some more wine, topping up their glasses.

'I've another fortnight. I come every year for three weeks—besides Christmas, that is. I spend Christmas here because I'm on my own.'

'You've no parents?'

'Both died when Melanie and I were small. We were brought up by an aunt, but she died three years ago, just after Melanie got married and came here.'

They chatted on for another hour, a pleasant hour of swiftly-developing friendship resulting in Rex saying in a firm inexorable voice,

'We mustn't lose touch, Laura. Let's exchange addresses now, before I walk you back to the Palacio. I've so thoroughly enjoyed this evening that I want a repetition.' A pause as he looked a trifle anxiously at her. 'You feel the same?'

She nodded without hesitation.

'Yes, Rex, I'd like to do it again.'

'We don't live too far from one another. I've a car, so the journey to Birmingham won't present any problems.' He was bringing out a notebook and soon the addresses were exchanged.

'I must go now,' said Laura, glancing at her watch. She was usually in her room by ten o'clock at night. It was now almost half-past. 'I don't want to find myself locked out!'

They walked back together; Rex left her at the gates of the Palacio, having agreed to meet her the following morning on the beach.

'I wonder if you'd care to meet my sister?' Rex looked expectantly at her, waiting for an answer.

'I don't know ...'

'Leave it until tomorrow.' He could see that she was restless, because it was so late. 'We'll talk about it then. Goodnight, Laura.'

'Goodnight, Rex.'

He opened one of the gates for her to pass through, then closed it again. She stood for a second or two, watching his departing figure, a warmth within her that she had not known since coming to Torassa.

She went quickly along the tree-lined pathway leading to the side door, which was off the larger courtyard. But to her dismay she realised that the Conde and Dona Eduarda were strolling in the moonlit garden and she had no means of escaping an encounter.

'Miss Conroy!' exclaimed Dona Eduarda with quite unnecessary loudness and surprise. 'What are you doing out at this time?'

Words that were bound to set Laura's hackles rising, mild-tempered though she was. She spoke her thoughts aloud, mindless of the Conde's presence.

'I wasn't aware that there was any set time for me to be indoors.'

Silence. Laura knew the Conde had stiffened, angered by the fact that anyone in her lowly position should speak in this way to his high-born guest.

'Have you been walking?' he inquired of her, his tones controlled but terse.

'Part of the time.' If he wanted to know more, then let him ask another question!

'And the other part, Miss Conroy?' He was standing some small distance from her, the Portuguese girl at his side. Lights all around provided more than enough illumination for Laura to see the arrogance on the faces of both of them. The girl, though, seemed to lack the nobility of the Conde; in consequence her arrogance seemed out of place. Moreover, there was hostility in her eyes, a sort of condescending sneer on her mouth.

'I've been to the café in town.' No more than that. Let him ask even another question. This he did, his eyes glinting dangerously.

'On your own, *senhorita*?'

Laura hesitated for a moment, and then,

'No,' she said with a trace of defiance, 'I was not on my own. I met one of my countrymen and we went to the café together.'

'You met——!' Dona Eduarda gasped. 'Do you mean, Miss Conroy, that you went to the café with a stranger—and stayed out until this time of the night?'

'What are you insinuating, madam?' Never had Laura known herself to become infuriated like this. She could have slapped the girl's face. 'Might I say that my actions are not your affair—and request that you keep your evil suspicions to yourself!' Laura would have moved on, for she was quivering with temper, but the Conde spoke, saying in his most icy tone of voice,

'*Senhorita*, please control yourself! Remember that you are speaking to my guest. How dare you insult her —and in my presence! You'll oblige me by making an immediate and sincere apology!'

Laura's eyes, those eyes which became so soft and limpid when she smiled, were blazing with fury, and her small hands were clenched tightly at her sides. Sheer undiluted rage flowed through every vein in her body, warming her blood until she felt some conflagration was burning within her. So new an experience! But one she could not control.

She turned on Dom Duarte and said quiveringly,

'Apologise? I think you're out of your mind even to suggest it! If anyone is entitled to an apology it's I! However, one would not expect so arrogant a person as your friend to possess the graciousness to apologise. I'll bid you goodnight, *senhor*!' And without affording either of them the chance to speak another word, Laura twisted round and ran across the lawn towards the house.

The following morning Laura awoke to the sound of birds singing, and to the perfumes of exotic flowers drifting into the room through the open window. For a fleeting moment she lay still, sublimely content, for everything was perfect. But then she jerked up and, getting out of bed, slipped into a negligée. The drapes were drawn back by the manipulating of a cord and she stepped out on to the balcony, her mind trying to accept the beauty, and to reject the ugliness of last night's scene, out there, in the Palacio gardens.

What an arrogant pair they were! A marriage between them would have been interesting to watch, for surely there would have been no warmth in it, no intimacy other than that of sex—and this, probably, only for the ensuring of an heir for the Conde.

Dismissing the two detestable people from her mind, she bathed and dressed, then rang the bell. Teresa appeared and Laura asked for her breakfast to be brought up to the balcony.

'Yes, of course, *senhorita*,' smiled the girl. 'Would you like tea or coffee?'

'Coffee, please. And only one slice of toast.'

'Yes. An egg, and one rasher of bacon?'

Laura nodded her head. She would be sorry to say goodbye to this charming girl.

It was over half an hour later when, having finished her breakfast, Laura was crossing the lawn on her way to the gate when she was called back by Gigo, who informed her that his master wanted to speak to her urgently.

Nerves became taut, then tingled, affecting her whole body. Should she refuse to obey this summons? The thought of an interview with the Conde was almost unnerving, as it was certain that he was going to give her the dressing-down of her life. Strange that she should experience fear when she knew she was not to be at the Palacio for more than about thirty hours, as her flight was scheduled for three-thirty the following afternoon.

'It's very important, *senhorita*,' said Gigo, seeing her hesitancy.

'Very well. Which room is Dom Duarte in?'

'The small drawing-room on the south side, *senhorita*.'

Two or three minutes later she was entering in answer to the curt 'Come in' which she had received immediately upon knocking quietly at the door. The Conde, clad in casual slacks of an attractive slaty blue and an open-necked shirt of the same colour but a much lighter shade, looked as austere and coldly impersonal as ever. His height, noticeable even in this lofty room, seemed to be accentuated by the position in which he stood, for he was by the white velvet drapes, with one slender brown hand casually holding the gold tassel which normally hung down at the side, and which was attached to the cord that opened and closed the drapes.

'You wanted to see me?' Laura's voice was quiet but firm, although deep down inside she was trembling, a circumstance that angered her, as she had come here determined not to be browbeaten by the high-handed lord of Torassa.

'It's concerning last night, Miss Conroy,' he began in that accented voice which, decided Laura after she had heard it a few times, could have been very attractive indeed, had its inflection not been so edged with cold hauteur. 'On thinking about it carefully I have come to the conclusion that there might have been more to the situation than appeared on the surface.' Here he paused, subjecting Laura to the most intensive scrutiny. It was as if he would read what was behind those serious grey-green eyes of hers ... and the second impression she had was that it was *important* to him to discover what she was thinking. 'Perhaps you have some explanation——' He stopped abruptly and to her amazement rephrased the query. 'Perhaps you had some excuse for your conduct towards Dona Eduarda?'

Laura could only stare, wondering what it had cost him to speak in this way. It would have been so much simpler to have ignored the whole distasteful business, especially as she was to leave within the next few hours.

'I would rather not say anything.' She spoke after a time of considering, her first impulse being to blurt out the truth and let him know that the precious Dona Eduarda had told an untruth about her. However, this

82

impulse was repressed, as Laura could find no gain in such a denouncement. 'I shall be leaving here very soon, Dom Duarte, so I think it is best that we do not trouble ourselves with what happened last night.' Her voice was low, and not too steady at all. She was reflecting on what might have been had the incident in the sea not have taken place. The Conde had wanted to read her notes on his pictures; she had been optimistic in that she felt he would be so impressed that he would then ask to take a look at her testimonials. The result, she knew for sure, would have been that she could restore one of his paintings. The chance was hers; she had only to prove herself and then all the other work would have followed. A sigh escaped her, but she did not speak, merely waiting for the Conde's response to what she had already said to him.

'The very context of your words is in itself mystifying, Miss Conroy. It increases my suspicions that there was something of which I am still in ignorance?' A question, which Laura ignored.

'You did hear the insinuation which Dona Eduarda made,' she said.

'I feel that, in the mood of the moment, you were far too hasty in jumping to conclusions. Dona Eduarda told me afterwards that she did not mean anything derogatory——'

'Senhor,' interrupted Laura, quite unable to let him go on, 'you are a perceptive man, obviously, so you must have known that my imagination was not running away with me. Dona Eduarda hinted that I and the young man I was with did not come straight home from the café. I am telling you that we did—although why I should take the trouble I don't know,' she added as he was about to interrupt her. 'It's of no importance to me whether or not you approve of my morals!'

The steely grey eyes widened for a second, then narrowed to mere slits. Laura, her temerity amazing her, for the man was indeed forbidding, looked directly at him and said stiffly that she had nothing more to say to him. She was meeting the young man she had been with last night, she did add as a parting shot before, with a frigid little bow that might have been more suited to the Conde himself, she made her way to the door and, opening it noiselessly, passed through and closed it just as noiselessly behind her.

Rex was waiting on the beach, his eyes lighting up when he saw her coming towards him along the sands. It was a perfect morning, with the tropical sunshine painting the calm blue waters and the pure white sand of the beach.

'I've brought a mac for us to sit on,' he told her eagerly as she reached him. 'How's the head?'

'Better. I don't feel a thing now.'

'Will you discard the bandage before you leave here?'

'Yes; the doctor said this morning that he would be replacing it tomorrow with a small dressing.'

'He's coming to the Palacio tomorrow, before you leave for the airport?'

'Yes, so he said. It doesn't matter if he doesn't, though. I shall be seeing my own doctor on Tuesday.'

Rex spread the mackintosh and they sat down.

'It's such a pity that you're leaving,' he said flatly.

'I'd like to have stayed—under different circumstances.'

'If you would care to come with me to see my sister——' he began, but Laura, guessing at once what was in his mind, interrupted to say quite firmly that she would not be able to accept an invitation to remain on the island.

'The Conde would certainly not like it,' she ended.

'It's got nothing to do with the Conde.'

'He does own this island.'

'Perhaps, but not those who reside on it.'

'Your sister and her husband are friends of the Conde,' Laura reminded him. 'It wouldn't be the thing for me to move from the Conde's home to theirs. Besides, you seem to have forgotten that I came here under false pretences in the first place.'

Rex gave a sigh.

'I suppose you're right,' he conceded, and then, 'But there's nothing to stop you from meeting my sister and her husband, is there?'

'No,' she agreed, 'there isn't.'

'Okay! Shall we go now?'

She had to smile at his boyish eagerness.

'If you like,' she said.

'It's about half an hour's walk if we go back and use the road, but, as you know, it'll take much less time if we use the beach.'

'I don't mind the beach.'

'It's so stony farther along.' Rex looked doubtfully at her rather flimsy sandals. 'Will you be all right?'

'Certainly I will. I've walked along there several times since I've been on the island.'

The house—a palacette with a fine Baroque façade and exotic gardens—was like a miniature of the Conde's great palace. The girl who came out on seeing Rex and his companion from the window was tall and slender and extraordinarily pretty. Fair-haired and blue-eyed, she had a smile as charming as her looks. She was coming down the steps by the time Rex and Laura reached them. They waited until she was at the bottom and then Rex made the introductions, adding, for his sister's benefit, just a few details as to the reason why Laura was here.

'So you met only last evening?' The girl waved a hand, a welcome invitation to enter the house. She preceded them up the steps. 'And you're leaving tomorrow. What a shame. Rex's one grumble about Torassa is that he's so much on his own. Not that he need be,' she went on with a glance over her shoulder, 'he will wander for miles and miles, so he can't expect either Pedro or me to accompany him. We both hate walking. If he'd stay around the house he wouldn't be so much on his own.'

The room into which she took them was delightfully furnished, with crimson velvet chairs and sofas and antiques shining with the patina of age. A crystal chandelier hung from the ceiling and there were wall lights and a standard lamp to match.

'Sit down, Laura,' invited Rex. And, more quietly, he asked, 'How does it compare with the Palacio?'

'Much smaller, of course, but just as charming.'

'Melanie hasn't yet got over her good fortune in marrying into the Portuguese nobility, have you?' He smiled affectionately at his sister, who had remained by the door, ringing the bell for a maid.

'We did marry for love, though,' she told Laura with a laugh.

'There aren't many Portuguese on this island,' Rex said for Laura's benefit. 'Just the Conde, Pedro, and two other families.'

Laura was nodding. Teresa had mentioned this already.

'Do you have much social life?' she asked.

'All we need. Pedro and I are a quiet, homely couple. We're fond of each other's company.'

86

'If you're in love,' commented Rex amusedly, 'you don't need any social life.'

'It wouldn't do for you to live on Torassa, Rex.' His sister sat down on one of the small sofas and looked at Laura. 'How would you take to the isolation?' she asked with a smile.

'This life would suit me,' Laura confessed. 'I love the quiet, the cleanliness, the lack of crowds and traffic. I think it's heavenly.'

'Very different from Birmingham,' said Rex with a grimace.

'Indeed yes——' Laura broke off as the door opened and a maid appeared. Melanie said something to her in Portuguese and the girl went out of the room again. Within two or three minutes a man entered, a man of average height, dark of skin and with the sort of large brown eyes that any woman would have found attractive in that they were soft and affectionate—like those of a faithful dog.

Pedro came forward with a smile and was introduced to Laura. His grip was firm, his voice friendly when he spoke.

'I'm happy to meet you, *senhorita*. It isn't often we have a pretty English girl visit us here on Torassa. You're with friends?'

Laura explained, helped now and then by an intervention from Rex.

'So you came to restore those paintings? I remember how they came to be damaged. It was when they were taken down when the gallery was redecorated. Someone —Duarte never did find out who—stored them in a loft where there was a loose tile——' He stopped, frowning in concentration. 'Ah, yes, I remember, the tile had blown off, leaving a hole in the roof, and when we had one of our tropical storms the rain really did get into that loft. Duarte didn't know that his precious paintings had been put up there—obviously it must have been one of the workmen, moving things around the way they do. He was furious, and a man did come in to do a little work on them, but of course they require an expert.' He looked at Laura in some doubt. 'You believed yourself capable of restoring them to their former beauty?'

'Definitely, *senhor*. I know I can do this work to the entire satisfaction of the Conde.' There, let Pedro repeat what she had said. It would serve the Conde right if, later, he regretted allowing her to have a try.

Refreshments were brought in by the maid. Laura enjoyed the conversation but refused an invitation to stay for lunch. She felt she had not known Melanie and Pedro long enough to accept that kind of hospitality. Rex was plainly disappointed, but that made no difference to Laura.

'I'll take you back to the Palacio,' he was offering later, though his voice was unenthusiastic. 'I'll be back in about an hour,' he added, speaking to his sister.

At the Palacio gates he asked Laura if she would see him that afternoon.

'I ought to do some packing,' she began, but Rex interrupted her, persuasively declaring that there would be plenty of time the following morning to do her packing. She had to smile, and presently she said,

'All right, Rex, I'll meet you this afternoon.'

'Fine!' His face lit up. 'I'll be strolling along the beach after lunch.'

She nodded. It didn't seem necessary to state a time, since the beach was almost always deserted, so there was no possibility of their missing one another.

Immediately she entered the Palacio Clara came forward from the direction of the small sitting-room which seemed to have been given over to Marianna and the child for their private use.

'Miss Conroy ...' The child looked up into her face in a conspiratorial way that brought a frown of puzzlement to Laura's forehead. 'The pictures ... I've scratched two of them, so that they need mending. Uncle Duarte will have to let you stay now, won't he?'

'You've scratched two pictures!' Laura felt something lodge in her throat; it caused a hollowness to creep into her voice. Her heart was beating far too quickly, her mind searching desperately for some way of covering up what the child had done. 'Clara, you're a very naughty girl!'

'Naughty? I was doing it for you, to make up for telling that lie. You can now say to my uncle that you've been looking at the pictures, and have found two that really do need mending. He'll let you stay and mend them!' Clara's eyes were bright, her small face animated. It was as simple as that—to a child's mind, of course.

'I'll go and see these pictures.' Laura looked into the upturned face, trying to see the situation through the child's eyes, and it was easy to establish the picture. Clara really believed she was making amends. But on the other hand, she had done deliberate damage to her uncle's paintings, and for that she deserved to be punished.

'Can I come with you?' Clara's voice pleaded, but Laura shook her head.

'No, Clara, you can't. Go back to Marianna, at once.' The child's face fell.

'I want to come with you, to show you what I've done.'

'It isn't necessary.'

'But you don't know which pictures they are.'

'I shall soon find them,' returned Laura grimly.

And she did, one with a scratch that had almost broken the canvas, the other with a longer scratch but which did not go as deep. Filled with dismay, Laura felt that she herself was indirectly responsible for this act of vandalism, since if she had never come here none of this could possibly have happened.

What a lot of trouble she had caused the Conde, reflected Laura unhappily. If only she had acted with more wisdom and maturity.

That he would be absolutely furious went without saying. Clara would be well and truly punished, while Laura would receive another dressing-down. What a mess! Laura examined the first painting carefully, trying to estimate just how long it would take her to put it right. Days, she thought with a deep sigh, as there were five colours involved. Each would have to dry before she could begin using another.

A sound behind her caused Laura to swing round, her heart giving a great lurch.

'Clara!' she almost snapped. She had fully expected to see the Conde standing there, aghast at the damage done to his precious works of art. 'I told you to go back to Marianna!'

The child's face was pale, her small hands clenched.

'I forgot to ask you not to tell my uncle that it was I who had scratched the paintings.'

'I have no intention of telling him.' Laura's voice was still sharp even though she was acutely aware of the child's anxiety. 'However, you do realise that he's going to make an inquiry?'

'Inquiry?' Clara obviously did not understand, and Laura explained. 'Oh, well ... he'll think it was one of the maids, but he'll not be able to find out which one ...' Clara's voice trailed away to silence as Laura's fixed gaze became even more stern than before. 'Please don't tell him it was me!' Clara's voice had risen; tears had leapt to her eyes. Laura's sternness dissolved. The child had meant well, had wanted Laura to be permitted to stay and repair the paintings.

'Go back to Marianna,' she said wearily. 'I shan't say a word to your uncle, so you needn't worry about it.'

'Thank you,' said Clara, and went off, beginning to trot along the length of the gallery. Laura drew a breath. A charming child, but in need of some discipline, that was for sure!

CHAPTER SIX

ALTHOUGH she went out after lunch to meet Rex, Laura felt she could have been better occupied in trying to do something to the one painting, at least—the one whose damage was not so great. True, the actual scratch was longer than the other, but it was not anywhere near as deep. Given enough time without interruption she could do a fairly good job on that painting. But there was of course the risk of someone's coming up to the gallery and finding her there, engaged on work which the Conde had refused to allow her to do. Should the Conde himself catch her touching his paintings, then she *would* be in trouble! Laura shivered at the thought, but the next moment was wondering what would happen when, after she had gone, Dom Duarte discovered the damage. Clara said he would blame one of the maids, but that was most unlikely. He would know very well that none of them would do a thing like that. Would he suspect Clara? Perhaps, and if she was questioned by her uncle it was fairly certain that the child would be forced to tell him the truth.

'You look troubled about something, Laura.' Rex's voice, tinged with concern, broke into her musings and she turned towards him, a faint smile appearing on her lips.

'It's nothing,' she returned airily. 'Shall we walk towards the caves?'

'If you like.'

It was an hour and a half later that, having walked the length of the beach and then directed their steps towards the café, Rex asked Laura to dine out with him that evening.

'We could book the table while we're here,' he suggested. They were sitting outside, under the shade of a jacaranda tree, waiting for their cool drinks to be brought out to them by the smiling, tawny-skinned waitress.

'I'd like that,' murmured Laura, half her mind still on those damaged paintings.

'We'll meet around seven-thirty?'

'That'll suit me fine.'

She returned to the Palacio in time for a late afternoon tea, which Teresa brought up to her and set out daintily on the verandah table.

'Is there anything else?' she asked smilingly.

'No, thank you, Teresa.' Laura glanced at the table as she spoke. 'I shan't be having an evening meal,' she added as the girl was about to leave her. 'I'm going out to the restaurant for it.'

The girl's eyes widened and it did seem that she would for once forget herself and ask a question. However, she remembered just in time and, merely nodding, went from the verandah into the room behind. Laura poured herself some tea, ate a warm, home-made cake, and then, rising, she went along to the Gallery. It was as if she were moved by a compulsion beyond her own control. It was not surprising, though, she told herself, that she should be so concerned about the damage done by Clara.

'If only I dared to put a brush to this!' She traced the line of the scratch with her forefinger. 'I could do the blue,' she murmured, 'then the green ...' These would dry overnight, and tomorrow morning, very early, she could get up and come along to do the shading around these two colours. How deep was the scratch exactly? she wondered, taking off her brooch with sudden decision. The pin was carefully put into the crack——

'Miss Conroy! What are you doing?' The voice of the Conde was like an avalanche of ice enveloping her whole body; she wheeled around, the brooch falling from her shaking fingers. 'How dare you!' He strode towards her and stared at the painting, almost unable to believe his eyes. 'So ...' The aristocratic voice was very quiet now, dangerously quiet. 'For spite you would commit an act of vandalism, leaving it till the last moment, almost, so that it would not be detected until you had left my home.' The suppressed fury was revealed in the dark glint of his eyes. 'You despicable woman!' he added, those eyes fixing hers until, unable to stand his contempt any longer, Laura averted her head. 'Get out of here,' he ordered, pointing towards the door. 'And keep out ...' The harsh, accented voice trailed away to silence and even without looking up Laura knew that the worst had happend. His eyes had lighted on the other picture.

Laura's heart was throbbing wildly as she watched him take the couple of strides which brought him opposite to the lovely painting. She held her breath, almost unable to hold on to her secret, and yet so great was his fury that she could not bring herself to give the child away. Clara had said he would have spanked her for lying. What then would he do to her for committing damage like this? Laura had already guessed that there was a cruel streak within him. Laura watched him put out a finger and touch the canvas where it was almost ripped through. She could sympathise with him, being a lover of art herself. He must be feeling dreadful, seeing his precious oil painting so flagrantly damaged. If only she could explain, make him see that

Clara had meant well—— But no, that was mere wishful thinking, Laura told herself. Besides, she had already promised Clara she would not mention her act to the Conde.

He turned, and Laura realised—not without a sudden surge of anger—that her whole inside was a-quiver with apprehension. It was almost as if she were prepared for him to do her some physical injury! He stood, immobile, looking at her across the small distance separating them. Laura swallowed hard, cursing herself for the deep concern that had been responsible for her coming here in the first place. She could at this moment be on her verandah, finishing her tea in the sunshine, and with the song of the birds for company instead of this arrogant nobleman with the stern forbidding countenance and air of contemptuous accusation. Laura felt like a criminal facing her judge.

'Have you anything to say, Miss Conroy?' The softly-spoken question came at last, breaking the unearthly silence that had fallen on the Gallery. Laura shook her head, and glanced around almost wildly. Every face looking out from the canvases seemed to be stern and accusing.

'No, nothing,' she answered through stiff and whitened lips. She stooped to retrieve her brooch, and stared down at it, fumbling to fasten the pin. 'No ...' She repeated, and lowered her head still further, afraid to look him in the face.

'I have never known anything so petty!' The Conde's scathing simplicity of speech was to Laura a hundred times more cutting than a violent outburst would have been. She felt a cloud of tears behind her eyes, wondered why the Conde's contempt was so very painful. It seemed to touch a hidden chord so sensitive that she had never before known it existed. Miserably she turned away, desiring only to escape. She heard herself say, 'I'm sorry ... very sorry,' apologising for something she had not done. The Conde made no reply, but stood immobile, watching her retreating figure. She felt his gaze following her until she had passed through the high wide doorway. It seemed to burn into her back. She closed the door and then the tears came, so that she stumbled along the corridor and almost collided with the tall self-assured woman approaching in the opposite direction.

'Gracious, girl!' exclaimed Dona Eduarda crossly, 'where do you think you're going? You could have trodden on my feet!'

Something within Laura caught fire and her eyes blazed.

'Need you be so downright rude about it?' she cried. 'It seems to me that you have no idea what good manners are!'

'Why, you——!' The Portuguese girl glowered at her. 'Manners you say! If this is the way you conduct yourself in England then thank heaven I shan't ever be going there!'

Laura walked away, aware that the Conde had come to the door of the Gallery and was listening to this angry interchange. She heard Dona Eduarda say,

'That English girl's the limit, Duarte! It will be a good thing when she's gone.'

'I couldn't agree more, Eduarda.'

Had they spoken in English on purpose, so that Laura could understand? She rather thought so, but also admitted that they could have spoken automatically in English, since it seemed to be used here almost as much as Portuguese. With the natives of the island Portuguese was scarcely used at all by many of them,

their official language having been English long before
the family of Mauredo had come to settle here.

'Laura, there's something very wrong. Can't you con-
fide in me?' Rex spoke as he and she were sitting at
their table in the restaurant, waiting for the waitress to
come for their order. 'I noticed this morning that you
were troubled,' he went on to remind her, 'and I mentioned it but you insisted it was nothing and I didn't
like to pursue the matter.'

She looked at him, noting his frank open face, his
anxious eyes. His friendliness was like a soothing balm
to her and although she suspected she might regret it,
she found herself saying,

'It's the Conde—he's so unfriendly. Then there's that
awful Dona Eduarda, his girl-friend. She's so arrogant
with me.' A deep sigh escaped her. 'I have myself to
blame, of course,' she admitted wretchedly. 'I oughtn't
to have come, deceiving the Conde as I did.'

'He's unfriendly?' frowned Rex. 'Because of what
you did?'

'That, and other things.'

'Eduarda's a strange one, according to my sister,
who's met her once or twice. She was practically engaged to Dom Duarte at one time, but then she married
someone else. The Conde didn't appear to be very upset, according to what people told Melanie, and now
he's obviously interested in her again. She's very
wealthy, so Dom Duarte's probably as interested in her
money as he is in her.'

Laura frowned at this idea.

'I can't see Dom Duarte wanting any more money,
Rex,' she said.

'These rich aristocrats are always wanting more. It
always puzzles me why they should, but you've only to

look at some of our own nobility, and the way they enter into business—not one business but many, just to increase their wealth. Then they die and leave it and the State takes the lion's share.'

Laura said nothing to this; she was not particularly interested in such things. Her mind was elsewhere, with Dom Duarte, for although she told herself she disliked him, she could not deny that his appeal as a man had affected her profoundly, and it was still affecting her. She found excuses for his treatment of her because, quite reasonably, she saw the situation from his point of view. She had been accused of several disreputable actions which she had not made any attempt to deny having done. If she refused to vindicate herself then she had no right to expect anything else but the Conde's contempt. In his eyes she was guilty of these acts and therefore it was only to be expected that he would look down upon her with disgust, and at the same time wish she had never set foot on his island.

'You're miles away, Laura.' Rex spoke softly, persuasively, as if inviting her confidence. She merely smiled, relieved that the waitress had appeared with her little notepad on which she was ready to write down their order.

'We must have the fish,' Rex declared. 'It's so wonderfully fresh here, on Torassa.'

'Being caught each day, I suppose?' Laura had already decided that the fish caught around the coast of the island was the best she had ever tasted.

'Yes, indeed.' Rex gave the order, which came within a quarter of an hour. Laura enjoyed the meal, and the wine that went with the excellent food, but all the time she was thinking of Dom Duarte, and wondering how he was feeling about those damaged pictures. They would need so much care ever to be restored to their original beauty, although Laura felt she could have camouflaged the one so that it would scarcely have been noticed—at least, by an inexperienced eye or at a casual glance. Given more time, she knew she could put both paintings right again. Oh, well, it was not to be, and she hoped that the Conde would eventually find someone who could do the work to his entire satisfaction.

She was ready to leave, her suitcases packed and taken down to the hall, thence handled by Martim who was driving her to the airstrip. There was no sign of the Conde, and it suddenly occurred to Laura that he might not be intending to say goodbye to her even. Her feelings about this were mixed, as while on the one hand it would be a relief to leave without having to speak to him again, she felt a tinge of regret that she could not have one last word with him.

'It is time, *senhorita*,' Martim said presently. 'We must not be late.'

'No ...' She glanced around as she came from the Palacio steps towards the car. All was so lovely, so tranquil in the tropical sunshine. The sea, plainly visible from one particular aspect, was smooth, and dark turquoise in colour. The statues in the gardens shone in the golden light, the fountain sprayed a myriad lovely colours high into the air, a rainbow in miniature. As Laura got into the car an emerald green humming-bird flew past her and hovered over a flaring crimson hibiscus blossom, while another flew over to a huge morning-glory bush, darting about from side to side, its long curving beak ready to take the nectar from the flowers.

She gave a deep sigh and leant back against the soft upholstery of the car. This, then, was the end of her trip. An experience, she would always be able to tell herself ... but one which she never again wished to experience!

'We are here, *senhorita*.' Martim's quiet respectful voice was heard as he opened the door for her to alight. The aeroplane was there, but scarcely anyone was about. Laura felt she might be the only passenger leaving the island of Torassa.

She watched her luggage being taken away, then went across to the waiting lounge. Only another day and she would be home. The plane was touching down at several other places on the way, and Laura knew she would be impatient at the various delays.

Eventually she was on the plane, with only three others, all of whom were already aboard when the plane touched down on the Torassa airstrip. The engines turned—and it was at that very moment that she became aware of some unusual activity on the airfield. A car had slid to a standstill, a car which she knew belonged to the Conde, a small sports model which he always drove himself. Fascinated, Laura watched to see who he was rushing to the airport at this late stage. To her amazement he alighted and she saw that he had been the lone occupant of the car. An official was approached, and spoken to; both he and the Conde glanced towards the aeroplane. The official pointed, then came quickly across the intervening space. Laura saw his head appear, heard him say,

'Miss Conroy, will you please come off the aeroplane. Dom Duarte has given orders.

'C-come off?' Laura's heart gave a sickening lurch. What else had happened? What had Clara done now? 'But I don't want to come off,' she said presently, having gathered her resources sufficiently for her to defy the noble lord of Torassa. The plane would take off in a short while, she decided, and she had no intention of missing it.

'Dom Duarte's orders,' said the man, registering amazement at her defiance. 'Please—this way.'

Laura remained where she was.

'There is nothing important——'

Senhorita,' broke in the official impatiently, 'you will please do as Dom Duarte says!'

Laura's gaze had caught the Conde's tall figure as she looked through the window. He was staring at the official who was at the top of the steps. Obviously the illustrious nobleman had never been kept waiting before! His every wish had been deferred to, Laura had noticed during her stay at the Palacio; he was treated like a king.

'Tell him, please, that there is no reason at all why I should come off this plane. It will be away within a few minutes and I don't intend to miss it.'

'This aeroplane will not take off until the Conde gives his permission,' returned the official coldly. 'I can assure you, Miss Conroy, that his orders will have to be obeyed, so please do as I ask, and obey this order that he gives you.'

With a sigh of resignation Laura left her seat and went towards where the official was standing. She knew she had no alternative than to obey the Conde's order, simply because now that it had been brought to her notice, she knew for sure that the pilot dared not leave the airport until given permission to do so by the owner of the island.

'What do you want with me, sir?' The last word slipped out, as it had once or twice before, and a frown came to the Conde's forehead. However, he was plainly not concerned with such trivialities as a mere slip of the tongue on Laura's part. His face was set and severe, and a muscle moved strangely at the corner of his mouth.

'*Senhorita*,' he said sternly, 'it is my wish that you return to the Palacio. I have some things to discuss with you——'

'But——'

'I believe I have informed you, *senhorita*, that I do not tolerate interruptions.' So stiff! So austere, with that fixed expression in his steely grey eyes, and that taut jawline and inflexible mouth. 'You will get into my car, if you please.' He gestured arrogantly, and fully expected instant obedience. Laura said, examining the set mask of his face and discovering nothing from it,

'Will you not give me some clue as to why I must return to the Palacio, Dom Duarte?'

His gaze was still fixed—but oh, so very stern and accusing. Lord, what *had* the child done this time? she asked herself again.

'You, *senhorita*, have lied to me—on more than one occasion.'

Already she was shaking her head.

'But no, *senhor*——'

'Lied by your silence,' he almost snapped, and she saw how close he was to fury. 'Yes, lied by your silence! You will accompany me back to my home and let me have the truth. In, at once!' She was really given no option, as the Conde took her arm in a hurtful grip and propelled her into the seat. The door was slammed upon her, and soon the Conde was driving off the airstrip and into the tree-lined road outside it.

Laura, quivering all over, and with her thoughts rioting, endeavoured to fathom exactly what had happened. That this was futile soon struck her. Of one thing only could she be sure: the Conde had, somehow, discovered that it was not she who had damaged his paintings. Whether he knew the true facts about the other incident was not clear, but Laura was confident that she would very soon be enlightened as to that also.

They arrived at the Palacio very quickly indeed, the Conde having driven with quite staggering speed, this in spite of the narrowness of some of the roads. That he was in a temper went without saying, and Laura was more than once reminded of her previous conviction that he would never be in a fury. Well, that was one count on which she had made a mistake!

'In here,' commanded Dom Duarte immediately they entered the house. He gestured towards the Crimson Lounge, a lovely apartment tastefully furnished, and with high wide windows facing the sea. A fishing boat bobbed about on the aquamarine water; a surf-rider sped past it, sending spray high into the air. Perfumes from the gardens entered the room; a brightly-plumaged parakeet settled on the sill, then flew off again to be joined by its mate in a tall tamarisk tree.

'And now,' said the Conde through his teeth, 'you'll explain just why you concealed the truth about those pictures! Yes,' he added on seeing her expression, 'Clara's made a confession—after having made a slight slip which instantly aroused my suspicions!' His wrath consumed him and this made Laura ask,

'Have you been angry with Clara?'

An awful silence followed.

'Miss Conroy,' said Dom Duarte at length in a dangerously soft tone, 'will you answer my question!'

She felt her colour rise, with embarrassment rather than anger.

'I'm sorry,' she returned huskily. 'I was concerned, you see, about the child——'

'Answer my question!' he rasped, and Laura actually jumped.

'Yes, Dom Duarte,' she responded in some haste, and at the same time taking an involuntary step backwards. But then she found herself tongue-tied, unable to see how she could begin. 'The paintings——' she quivered, 'you th-thought that I'd damaged them, and—and I didn't blame you, sir——' She broke off, catching her underlip between her teeth. No doubt about it, this Portuguese Conde was disconcerting! 'Clara meant well, Dom Duarte,' continued Laura, wishing this choked sensation within her throat would clear so that speech would be made easier. 'You see, she wanted me to stay and restore the pictures—the original ones, I mean, and so—so she had the idea to——' Laura broke off, spreading her hands. 'I expect you've managed to get all this from Clara?' she ended on a slightly petulant note.

The steely grey eyes scarcely moved as the Conde replied,

'I wanted your version, Miss Conroy. Proceed, if you don't mind.'

'Proceed?' Her eyes, shy and clear, stared into his. 'But you know it all!' she exclaimed with a sort of desperation. 'I was just looking at the damage when you saw me with that brooch.'

'Not all,' was the Conde's quiet denial. 'For instance, I did say, if you remember, that there might have been some reason for your rudeness towards Dona Eduarda?'

So ... He suspected something, did he? His words also told Laura that although he knew about the paintings, he was still in ignorance of what actually happened when Clara went into the sea. Laura was not intending to enlighten him; she suspected that Clara was in enough trouble already. It was an undoubted fact that Laura would have derived extreme satisfaction from exposing Dona Eduarda, but not at the expense of the child.

'I don't know what you mean,' she said at length, not daring to look at him in case he should see instantly that she was lying.

He drew a breath but to her great relief allowed this matter to drop.

'I suppose,' he conceded after what seemed an eternity of thought, 'that you are to be commended for your reluctance to get Clara into trouble. Nevertheless,' he added in a frigid tone, 'I am exceedingly displeased. I like to think that I never misjudge people, and you, *senhorita*, have been the cause of my misjudging a person for the first time in my life!' He stopped; she noticed the threads of crimson creeping along the sides of his mouth. She swallowed nervously, waiting for his next words. They were scathing, they were denunciatory, they were harshly accusing.

Laura listened without speaking, convinced that it was better to let the Conde have his say to the full. In any case, she had been admonished more than once for interrupting him when he was speaking. He stopped at last; she drew a deep breath of relief. Her cheeks were hot, her eyes downcast. She supposed she ought to try and vindicate herself, now that the opportunity had come, but she very much feared that no matter what she might say in excuse for her silence, this man would denounce her conduct. He had already made the only concession he intended to make, which was that she was to be commended for her reluctance to give the child away.

She looked up at last, unable to bear the awful silence a moment longer, and asked respectfully if the plane would have waited for her.

'Certainly not!' was his brief reply.

'Then how am I to get away from here——?' She spread her hands helplessly, blinking rapidly in order to stem her tears. 'When is the—n-next flight?'

A long unfathomable pause followed and then, with what was obviously some considerable difficulty, the Conde spoke.

'I wish you to remain here and restore the two pictures which Clara damaged.'

Was she altogether surprised? It suddenly struck her that, had the Conde merely wanted to give her a good telling off, he had no need to fetch her back here in order to do so. He could have done it at the airport, then let her leave as arranged.

He had intended asking her to restore the paintings.

'I don't know,' she began uncertainly. 'They might be difficult ...'

'You gave me to understand that you were an expert,' the Conde reminded her smoothly.

She nodded.

'Yes.'

'Well then, what's the difficulty?'

She wanted to say that it wasn't the pictures that caused her hesitancy, but the atmosphere at the Palacio. She'd not been happy there. However, she did want to accept the Conde's challenge; she also wanted to put right the damage which Clara had done, because, naughty as the act was, the child had meant well, had hoped by her action that she was making amends for the lies she had told.

'I'll do them for you,' she agreed, and involuntarily she smiled, and her shy eyes became moist and limpid, a circumstance that attracted the Conde's whole attention for one fleeting moment before he said, in that cool and foreign voice of his,

'Anything you require will be provided, Miss Conroy. *Is* there anything special you require?'

Laura shook her head.

'I shall have to make some tests, but I have all the materials with me.'

'The work of restoration is extremely delicate,' he said knowledgeably, 'especially on those two which have been scratched.'

'Yes, indeed.'

'You said just now that you were looking at the damage. Was it your intention to make some effort at disguising the damage which Clara had done?'

'I thought I might do some minor repairs to the one which wasn't so deeply scratched,' she had to admit. 'But it would not really have passed muster if an expert had looked at it.'

His hard grey eyes were stern.

'I should have been angry indeed had you touched any one of my pictures without first asking my permission.' The Conde paused a moment, as if allowing Laura to digest this. 'I expect you will now make a thorough job of the restoration.' A statement even though it was spoken in the tone of a question. Laura answered that she would guarantee him a successful restoration of those two paintings. If he was satisfied, she thought there was a good chance of his asking her to do the rest, but of course she made no mention of this to the Conde; the time was definitely not right.

Within a couple of hours she was unpacked and comfortably settled again in her room. Teresa was delighted and made no attempt to hide that delight.

'So you will be here for some weeks at least?' she said.

'Yes, at least a month,' replied Laura with a smile. 'It will take at least that long to do the two paintings.'

'And the rest?'

'I don't know about those yet,' replied Laura with a rueful inflection. 'It all depends on whether or not I satisfy Dom Duarte with these first two.'

'He's very hard to please,' stated Teresa with a shake of her dark head. 'You see, *senhorita*, he's a perfectionist.'

'I know that,' returned Laura wryly. 'I can only do my best and hope that it will be good enough.'

Marianna had up till now had little to do with Laura, but later, when Laura was changing for dinner—the Conde having sent word up by Teresa that he would expect her to dine with him and Dona Eduarda —she knocked on Laura's bedroom door and entered in answer to her invitation.

'I feel I ought to apologise for Clara's naughtiness,' she began without preamble, and in excellent English. 'I blame myself, in a way, because I have allowed her to run from me, several times.' The girl seemed distressed, thought Laura, hastening to reassure her.

'It doesn't matter now,' she smiled, feeling sorry for the girl. It couldn't be easy, keeping a continuous watch on a child as lively and venturesome as Clara. 'I rather think that Clara will be a little subdued for the next week or so.'

Marianna's eyes opened wide.

'More than a week or so!' she declared. 'Her uncle severely chastised her, and threatened even more if she got into any further scrapes while she is with him.'

Laura said,

'Do her parents tend to spoil her a little? Is that what's wrong?'

'They do spoil her, yes. She's the only child, you see, and it would be better if she had a brother or sister, I think.'

'Yes, I agree.'

'When she comes here it's so different for her; she has to behave.'

Laura did not doubt that, but said no more on the subject. Marianna, seeing that she was glancing anxiously at the clock, withdrew quietly and Laura was able to continue with her dressing. She had been surprised by the invitation and she now wondered what Dona Eduarda would think about having her dine with her and Dom Duarte. That she would not be pleased went without saying.

Laura at last picked up the comb and ran it through her luxurious hair. The colour had come up brighter than ever, the result of a new shampoo she had used that morning. Her dress of white broderie anglaise over a turquoise underskirt was a dream—so Avice had said on first seeing it. Laura liked it too and by the time she was on her way down to the dining-room she felt she had never looked more attractive than she did this evening. The dressing on her temple, though not very large, did show, but even to Laura's critical eye it was by no means unsightly enough to mar her appearance. Her rosy lips formed a ready smile when on entering the room she encountered Dom Duarte, superb in a dinner jacket and snow-white shirt. Her cheeks glowed with healthy colour, her hair shone, as did her eyes, and she felt the Conde's eyes staying on her rather longer than was usual. And they flickered in the strangest way. If only Dona Eduarda were not here ... What was she thinking about? Laura asked herself; it could make no difference at all if the Portuguese girl was not here ... or could it? Those occasions when she and the Conde had dined alone were rather wonderful, even though he was aloof and she often shy and unsure of herself.

'A drink, *senhorita*?' His voice was not so austere as usual and she wondered if he were in a forgiving mood.

Yet immediately on this idea was the sharp reminder that although he now knew it was Clara who had damaged the pictures, there was still much he did not know. For instance, he still believed that she, Laura, had tempted Clara to go into the sea; he still believed that she had meant to abandon the child, swimming for safety herself. But he *had* once said that perhaps Laura had some reason for her rudeness towards Dona Eduarda, reflected Laura thoughtfully, and wondered if the Conde with his shrewdness of mind had had an idea that there was another aspect to that incident. No, she decided. The Conde's instinct would surely be to believe the girl whom he knew, who was his friend. He would never expect her to lie. Why, then, had he spoken those words about Laura having a reason for her rudeness towards the Portuguese girl? With an inward sigh of resignation Laura owned to herself that her question was unanswerable. In any case, the Conde was speaking again, asking which drink she preferred.

'You'll be making a start on the pictures tomorrow morning, I presume?' he was saying with cool politeness after handing Laura her drink.

'I'll be busy with the tests, yes.'

'Take your time,' he said. 'I want perfection; nothing else matters.'

Laura sipped her drink, wishing the Conde would sit down; his height always overpowered her.

Dona Eduarda was taking a long time to get dressed, thought Laura, glancing at the wall-clock. Dom Duarte appeared not to mind in the least that the Portuguese girl was not here. He chatted for a few minutes with Laura about the pictures, and it seemed incredible that, only a few hours earlier, she had received from his scathing lips the most severe telling off of her life.

'Tell me about your father,' he invited, taking

possession of a chair at last. 'I am sorry I could not have him here at the time I wrote. He was a very clever man, so I was informed.'

'Very clever. He loved old paintings; he passed this love on to me.' Laura's shy grey-green eyes met the Conde's, then were hidden as her lashes came down. 'I'm most fortunate in being given this—er—reprieve, if one could call it that.'

'Perhaps,' murmured Dom Duarte unexpectedly, 'we shall both be fortunate. I certainly shall consider myself so if you do in fact make a good job of my paintings. I was impressed by the notes you made, and would like to see your testimonials, if you would let me have them some time?'

'Thank you, Dom Duarte!' Her eagerness was plain for him to see and a hint of a smile touched the corner of his mouth. 'I'm so glad that you are willing to take a look at them.'

'You sound proud of them?'

'I am, very proud of them.'

'Ah ...' Dom Duarte turned as Dona Eduarda entered the room. 'There you are.' His eyes wandered over the svelte figure, then settled on the girl's lovely, classical face. 'Let me get you a drink.' The Conde rose at once and went over to the cocktail cabinet. Dona Eduarda just stood for a long moment and stared at Laura as if she could not believe that she was really here. Without any attempt at tact she said,

'Is Miss Conroy dining with us, Duarte?'

'Yes,' he replied with a smile. 'As I mentioned to you earlier, Miss Conroy's going to restore those two paintings which were damaged by Clara.'

'I see.' The girl stared again, automatically accepting the glass which was being handed to her by Dom Duarte. Her face was a study, registering arrogance, disdain, superiority. But there was something else altogether, a sort of envy, an invidiousness that went deep so that it was revealed in the hateful twist of the girl's mouth, the dark venom of her expression. Laura could actually *feel* this intense dislike which the girl had for her, could experience a prickling sensation running along her spine, affecting her nerves, her mind, her heart even.

'You appear to be displeased about something,' observed Dom Duarte as he stood beside the girl, looking down into her face.

'Me?' Dona Eduarda managed a light laugh. 'I'm far from displeased, Duarte,' she purred, and then, having drunk her aperitif very quickly, she asked Dom Duarte to pour her another.

He obliged. Laura discovered a charm about him this evening that affected her emotions profoundly. She wished again that the Portuguese girl was not here, wished that she and the Conde were dining alone ...

CHAPTER SEVEN

ALL through the meal Laura knew this charm, was affected by the Conde's every word, every turn of his head, every expression in his steely grey eyes. She was fully aware that the Portuguese girl was watching her, that she knew of the effect the Conde was having on her. There were occasions when, unnoticed by Dom Duarte, Dona Eduarda would send an almost venomous glance in Laura's direction and Laura would experience a great dampness of spirit at the idea of the Conde's marrying this girl, of spending the rest of his life with her. Dona Eduarda was, outwardly, beautiful, flawless in every way. Inwardly she was hard, unfeeling, mercenary. Surely Dom Duarte could see this? Perhaps, though, the girl's character was of far less importance than her beauty, as a man like the Conde Duarte André Volante de Taviro Mauredo would have to have a wife who would be an adornment to this fantastically beautiful palace, a woman who could act like a queen, for assuredly the Conde was a king, king of this lovely coral island of Torassa.

'*Senhorita*, you are not hungry?' The question came from the Conde; his eyes were on her plate.

Laura smiled and said,

'I was day-dreaming. I'm sorry if I wasn't attending to my food.' Was that the correct thing to say? Laura was always wondering if her manners and etiquette were correct, as living in a palace was far different from living in her small flat at home.

'Perhaps,' drawled Dona Eduarda, 'our food isn't to Miss Conroy's liking.'

'On the contrary,' returned Laura, 'I find your food delicious, especially the fish.'

'Ah, yes,' smiled Dom Duarte, 'our fish. It is caught each day, you see, and so it's always fresh. I expect you've tasted some kinds of seafood here that you've never tasted before?'

Laura nodded, trying to hurry with what was on her plate, conscious that the other two were waiting for her, as was the liveried footman standing behind the Conde.

'Yes, indeed. I had some delicious fish last evening at the café in town. I have forgotten the name——'

'You were in the restaurant last evening?' broke in Dona Eduarda. 'With your boy-friend?'

Colouring up, Laura said with a sort of stiff politeness that she did not have a boy-friend, either here or at home.

'The young man I was with is a visitor to Torassa; he's staying with his sister.'

'Yes, you've been going out with him, though.' A statement. Laura allowed her glance to travel to the Conde, sitting at the head of the table—like a feudal overlord with one of his vassals behind him, ready to obey his slightest command.

'I have been out with him once or twice,' admitted Laura, aware of anger rising within her. How long was the girl staying at the Palacio? she wondered ... wishing she would leave the very next day!

'Have you met his sister and her husband?' inquired Dom Duarte conversationally.

'Yes, Rex took me to their house.' Laura put down her knife and fork and leant back in her chair. The footman quietly removed the three plates, then put down three more.

'Pedro and his wife are very good friends of mine,'

said Dom Duarte. 'They will be my guests for dinner next Saturday.'

So Rex might visit the Palacio after all. Laura did not ask the Conde whether Rex was included, though; it would seem to be an impertinence on her part.

Later, the Conde asked Laura if she was quite happy with her room. His intention had originally been to give her father a suite, and this was available should she want it.

'You would have a sitting-room,' he added, 'that is the main difference.' He looked at her unsmilingly, waiting for her answer.

'I like my room,' she said. 'I'd rather keep it, if you don't mind?'

'I shouldn't think it necessary for Miss Conroy to have a suite,' remarked Dona Eduarda with the hint of a frown. 'After all, it *was* a *Mr* Conroy to whom you were giving the suite.'

The Conde, impassive, picked up his knife and fork. Laura wondered if Dona Eduarda grasped that she'd been snubbed. At least, Laura herself would have considered his action as a snub, had it been she who had interrupted with the irrelevancy about *Mr* Conroy. Looking at the girl, Laura did notice the merest hint of pink about her cheeks, but the next moment Dona Eduarda was talking to Dom Duarte about the ride they had had that morning.

'It was marvellous!' she exclaimed. 'The early morning air here on Torassa is something one has to experience, for it cannot be described.'

'A small piece of land surrounded by water is usually a place where the air is clear and fresh,' remarked the Conde. 'Do you ride, *senhorita*?'

'Not now,' replied Laura. 'When I was small I used to visit my grandmother, who lived in the country.

There was a riding-school at the end of the lane and she paid for lessons for me.'

'You enjoyed riding?'

'I loved it.'

'I have several horses in the stables; you are at liberty to ride one if you wish.'

Laura's shy eyes sparkled.

'Oh, thank you, Dom Duarte! Thank you very much.'

Her eagerness obviously touched a chord of amusement because a smile came to the corner of his mouth. Dona Eduarda, on the other hand, was frowning darkly and Laura knew without any doubt at all that she was displeased at the offer made by the Conde.

'See one of the grooms,' he was saying. 'He'll advise you about a suitable mount. If you haven't ridden much recently you'll not be wanting too lively an animal at first.'

'I'll do that,' returned Laura shyly. She smiled at him, and saw his interest being caught. The Portuguese girl's eyes slanted towards Laura, and in them there was something akin to actual hatred. Laura shivered, but became composed again instantly. For she was in a very happy state of mind because she was staying at the Palacio after all, and because the Conde was being nice to her ... and because of some new sensation in the region of her heart, a sensation which was quite beyond her understanding but which lifted her to such pleasurable heights that the slight tinge of fear that accompanied it passed her by almost unnoticed.

The main course, of pheasant, was cleared away, and over the soufflé the three chatted about the island, with the Conde, most gracious even though he remained unsmiling, telling Laura that she must now do some exploring.

'You will have your week-ends,' he added. 'Teresa can again act as your guide.'

What a change in the man, Laura was saying to herself much later when, having said goodnight to Dom Duarte and his friend, she went up to her bedroom to change her dress before taking a stroll in the palace grounds. The noble lord of Torassa was human after all, even though there remained a certain austerity about him that forbade any approach that might be called friendly. Had anyone ever progressed to the point of real intimacy with the man? Laura shook her head. He was too steeped in a consciousness of his own importance, of his noble ancestry, of the fact that here, on this island, his word and his alone was law. All obeyed him, all revered him. Laura wondered if he enjoyed this exalted position, or if he merely took it for granted.

In order to dismiss him from her thoughts she deliberately brought in a picture of Rex, and a smile involuntarily curved her lips. He was charming, and how glad he would be on hearing her news. He would want to meet her and go out with her, but she was determined to impress upon him that she would be fully occupied during the daytime and could not, therefore, meet him until the evening.

Clara and Marianna were at the stables when, on the following Saturday morning, Laura went over to look at the horses.

'Are you going to ride with us?' asked Clara, her eyes lighting up.

'Perhaps—if you want me to, that is?' Laura glanced at Marianna, to see that she was nodding and smiling.

'It would be very nice for the three of us to ride together,' she said.

'Will you be coming every morning?' Clara wanted to know, but Laura shook her head.

'Only on Saturdays and Sundays, Clara.' She looked down at the child, wondering if she had already forgotten about the lie she told. Laura wished that the Conde knew the truth about that incident, but the next moment she was thinking of the child. The Conde must never know. Laura dared not think about the punishment he had inflicted on Clara for damaging the pictures, for undoubtedly he would have shown her no mercy, child though she was.

The three rode away from the stables together; the Conde and Dona Eduarda were having breakfast on a small patio and the Conde waved as the three rode past in the distance. The Portuguese girl either did not notice them, or she chose to ignore them.

'Do you think my uncle will marry Aunt Eduarda?' asked Clara.

'I have no idea.' Laura felt her mouth go dry. 'Shall we go that way, through the Great Park?'

'Of course,' answered Marianna obligingly. 'We shall go wherever you would choose.'

Laura warmed to the girl, with her unspoiled charm, her dark prettiness and her obliging manner. However, Laura was not intending to ride in the Park unless Marianna really wanted to. And in fact she did manage to get it out of her that she would prefer to ride on the beach.

'Then it is the beach,' stated Laura firmly.

Marianna seemed taken aback at this spontaneous decision of Laura's to change her mind.

'Tomorrow we will ride in the Park,' she said, and this was agreed.

'If Aunt Eduarda and Uncle Duarte marry then I shall be a bridesmaid,' said Clara. 'Is it called that in

English?' she added, wrinkling her brow.

'Yes, that's correct. You do very excellently with your English, Clara.'

'Her parents have used two languages with her almost since she could talk,' put in Marianna. 'They believe that everyone should speak your language, as then they are understood almost wherever they might go.'

'Also, here on Torassa nearly everyone uses English all the time.'

'That's true,' agreed Marianna. 'The island used to be owned by one of your countrymen.'

'How long will it be, Marianna,' said Clara, 'before we know whether they will get married?'

'That's not a very sensible question, Clara.'

'You always know things. Why is it not sensible?'

'Because no one knows if your aunt and uncle will marry.'

'I heard my mama say that they nearly got married once before.'

'Watch where you're going,' warned Marianna as they went slowly along the beach. 'There are large lumps of coral here and there. Don't let Murani step on one of them.'

'You always change the subject when I speak of Aunt and Uncle getting married,' protested Clara with a frown. 'Miss Conroy, you tell me, please, if you think they'll get married soon.'

'I've already told you, I have no idea, Clara.'

'I'm glad they didn't get married once before,' went on Clara, undaunted by the answers she was receiving. 'Because I was too young to be a bridesmaid. I didn't like Uncle João anyway!'

'Hush! You don't say things about people who have died.'

'Aunt Eduarda does. She said she was sorry she'd married him.'

Marianna was uncomfortable and it showed. She sent a darkling glance in the direction of her charge, but it had little effect on that young lady.

'Shall we turn back now?' Laura suggested, hoping to divert the child's interest. 'We've ridden a long way.'

'Can't we go to the headland?'

'No, I think we shall turn back,' said Marianna.

'Can we come after lunch and swim in the lagoon?'

'Perhaps.'

They all turned around and cantered along the soft white sands, the fresh clean breeze from the Indian Ocean caressing their faces and teasing their hair. The Conde and Dona Eduarda were at the stables when they arrived back.

'Did you have a good ride?' he asked, his grey eyes taking in Laura's flushed cheeks and tousled hair.

'Yes, lovely, thanks!'

'I see that Nayrilla was chosen for you. Happy with the mount?'

'Very——' Laura, having dismounted, patted the horse's neck before the groom appeared to take it away. Another groom was saddling Burkan, a beautiful pure-bred Arab stallion, which the Conde invariably rode. 'She's a dream! So gentle . . .' Laura's voice trailed away as she became aware of her own enthusiasm. The Conde was always so stiff and impassive that any show of emotion seemed out of place. In a more demure voice she added, 'Thank you very much, Dom Duarte, for letting me have the horse.'

'A pleasure, *senhorita*,' was his cool but gracious rejoinder. His eyes wandered and he watched a third groom saddling Ludran, another Arabian pure-bred whom Dona Eduarda was going to ride.

Laura watched them both ride away, a superlative couple, both with the same aristocratic bearing, both riding incredibly beautiful horses. A tiny sigh escaped her; she felt restless and knew that it was the Conde who disturbed her. Out of reach though he was his influence affected her, set in motion a sort of yearning that was both incomprehensible and troublesome.

After lunch Laura went out to meet Rex on the beach. They swam in the lagoon, then sunbathed on the warm white sands with their fringe of palm trees behind which lay the lush green hills of the island.

'It's idyllic,' she murmured, feeling rather proud of the lovely golden tan she was swiftly acquiring.

'And romantic,' supplemented her companion. 'The perfect setting for a romance to start, in fact.'

Laura laughed, even though she was well aware that his words held a seriousness about them that was meant to reach her.

'I've made a good start on the Conde's paintings,' she said, stretching her legs luxuriously on the towel she had brought out with her from England.

'Work!' was Rex's scoffing rejoinder. 'I was talking of something far more interesting!'

'I came here to work,' she reminded him.

'But your work finishes on a Friday night and doesn't start again until Monday morning. This is Saturday afternoon.'

Again she laughed.

'Are you looking forward to the Conde's dinner party this evening?' she asked.

'Yes! Don't change the subject!'

'I'm not wanting romance, Rex.'

Rex frowned at her from his sitting position on another gaily-coloured towel.

'I have never heard the word "romance" spoken in so prosaic a manner,' he chided.

'Maybe I'm unromantic,' she suggested, her eyes wandering to the ship that had appeared on the horizon. Was it a cruise ship? she wondered. It certainly would not be calling here.

'You are not unromantic! Have you ever had a boy-friend, a serious one, I mean?'

Laura said no, she had always been far too busy with her work.

'It was busy enough when Father was alive,' she added, 'but it's even worse now that I have everything to do myself. I love my work, though. It's so absorbing.'

'As long as you don't allow it to become *all*-absorbing it'll be okay. All work and no play makes Jill a dull girl.'

'Am I dull?' she asked with feigned concern. Her thoughts flitted to the Conde. Did he consider her dull? she wondered ... and this time her concern was genuine!

'Certainly not!' Rex slid down and came closer to her. 'I could like you a lot, Laura,' he said.

'You'll be leaving here in less than a week,' she reminded him.

'What of it? We've already exchanged addresses and said we'd keep in touch.'

'Keeping in touch is all right, but as for anything else ...'

'Yes?' he prompted when her voice had faded.

'My work, Rex——'

'You could keep on with your work even if we were married.'

'Married?' Laura sat up rather suddenly. 'I'm not thinking of getting married, Rex.'

'No, that was silly of me,' he declared with an edge

of anger to his tone. 'I was way ahead, wasn't I?'

'A very long way ahead,' answered Laura seriously. 'We hardly know one another, Rex.'

'I feel as if I've known you for ages.'

Laura's gaze was fixed on the ship, a tiny matchbox toy in the vastness of the ocean, but her mind was on the illustrious owner of the Palacio de Mauredo, who many people expected would eventually marry the beautiful and sophisticated Dona Eduarda de Manso, a millionairess in her own right.

'Penny for them,' she heard her companion say, jerking her from her reverie.

'I was thinking of Dom Duarte and Dona Eduarda.'

'She's still at the Palacio?'

'Of course. You'll be meeting her this evening.'

'Hmm ... Will they announce their engagement, do you suppose?'

'Announce ...' Something icy rippled along Laura's back, erasing the sun's warmth. 'Why do you ask a question like that?'

Rex gave a shrug.

'Melanie seems to expect an early announcement, so I just had the idea that it might be made this evening.'

A silence followed. Laura felt her mouth go dry, just as it had this morning when Clara mentioned marriage between Dona Eduarda and the Conde. What was this sense of dejection, this dampness of spirit which assailed her? Why should she care if the two got married? Who was she to have any sort of opinion about the suitability of Dona Eduarda as a wife for Dom Duarte? Much less should she have the fixed opinion that he would be making a mistake in marrying her.

'I suppose—suppose it could be tonight,' she murmured at last.

'A dazzlingly beautiful girl, plus a million or so of

what makes life pleasant—he can't go wrong, can he? I don't know what the delay is for; it isn't as if she's only just been widowed. I think Melanie said that a couple of years have gone by since her husband died.'

Laura said nothing. The warmth had gone from her and even the sun's rays seemed brittle and cold. What *was* the matter with her? What caused this depression ... what *really* caused it?

And then, with the speed of a flash of lightning, the truth was sparked off in her brain.

'No ... no ...!' She refused to admit it, convinced herself that her mind was playing her tricks. Her one and only interest in the Conde Duarte André Volante de Taviro Mauredo was that he owned precious works of art which she was here to restore to their original condition of colour and beauty.

The guests had arrived and were in the Blue Lounge with their pre-dinner drinks. Laura, having been in some doubt as to whether or not she would be invited to dine with the Conde and his guests, found her feelings mixed when at last the invitation was brought to her by Teresa. It was an undeniable fact that a certain pleasure would be hers, if only because of the presence of Rex, but on the other hand Laura was not in the least looking forward to an evening in the company of Dona Eduarda. Of her flash of comprehension earlier she would not think. With a sort of fierce determination she thrust it from her consciousness; she was *not* in love with the Conde! *Not!* Hadn't she always been a sensible person, never desiring that which was out of reach? Hadn't she always been content with the idea that she would eventually marry someone of her own station in life, and of her own country? This Portuguese nobleman, an alien and an aristocrat, had no place at all in the picture she had developed regarding her future.

No, she most certainly was not in love with the man —and that was the end of that!

She took up a comb, drew it through her hair in a couple of final strokes, her big grey-green eyes taking in all that looked back at her from the mirror. Her dress of ivory organza was high at the neckline, tight at the waist, and very full from there down, flowing out at the hemline. The sleeves were long, each tightly gathered into a narrow wristband which was fastened with four small pearl buttons. No jewellery adorned her except a small bracelet that had been her mother's.

She entered the room shyly, hesitantly, her eyes seeking those of the Conde. How devastatingly handsome he looked!—superbly attired with a correctness that instantly proclaimed him to be a man of quality ... a man apart.

Melanie smiled and so did Pedro, while Rex just stared at Laura in admiration. Dom Duarte came forward a step or two to indicate a vacant chair.

'Senhorita, please sit down. I believe introductions are unnecessary.' He inquired what she would like to drink, then went to get it for her.

'You look ravishing!' declared Rex. 'Pedro, you said she was pretty—but what do you think now?'

'She's very beautiful,' he answered gallantly.

Laura coloured delectably, and it was at that moment that the Conde turned, the glass in his hand. He stood still, his cool grey eyes examining her. Dona Eduarda seemed to be having a little trouble with her breathing, for her chest was moving up and down far more quickly than was normal.

'Allow me to compliment you on that most charming

dress, Miss Conroy,' he said, and came forward with her drink.

'Thank you, Dom Duarte,' murmured Laura, wishing she was not suffering such a high degree of embarrassment. Praise, though, had always done this to her, even praise for her work.

Light conversation followed, with Rex monopolising Laura for most of the time. Dona Eduarda did speak to Laura once or twice, but there was always a coldness in her voice, and in her eyes an expression of superiority which to Laura was offensive. It seemed as if the girl were portraying disdain for one who was very far beneath her. Melanie was vivacious, her husband quiet and reserved. Strange, thought Laura after studying them for a while, how opposite personalities could find harmony together.

The dinner was announced eventually and they proceeded into the glittering dining-room where the long table was alight with many candles set in silver candelabra. There were individual flower arrangements as well as the large centrepiece of orchids and rare ferns. The crystal glass gleamed beside each cover, the cutlery shone, as did the cruets, all of which were of antique silver.

Laura was seated next to Rex, and although she listened with apparent attention to all he was saying, her eyes would keep on strayinig to the Conde, who seemed deeply interested in the woman on his right ... Dona Eduarda. Laura noticed the significant glances of Melanie and her husband, and knew again that sensation of depression at the thought of the engagement being announced. How could the Conde be attracted to a woman as cold as Dona Eduarda? Did he not desire affection in his marriage?

'Laura, you're dreaming again. You seem to make a

habit of it.' Rex's voice in her ear brought her eyes from the fixed position as she stared at the Conde's profile while he talked to Dona Eduarda.

'Sorry. Er—what were you saying?'

'Never mind. You've stopped dreaming and that's all that matters.' Rex paused a moment. 'See what I mean about those two? Thick as you like, aren't they? Must get married, both of them, so why not to each other?'

'Must get married?'

'The Conde to have an heir and Eduarda to regain the status of a married lady.'

'Surely they'll not marry for such flimsy reasons as those!'

'I don't consider wanting an heir as a flimsy reason for marrying,' returned Rex in some amusement. 'All wealthy people do it.'

Laura frowned and spoke to Pedro, feeling she must drag her thoughts away from this possibility of an announcement which she knew would only serve to increase her dejection.

The dinner was over at last and they all retired to the Blue Lounge for coffee and liqueurs. There were dainty sweetmeats too, and cigarettes for those who wanted them. Rex and Pedro lighted up, but not the Conde. Dona Eduarda had her own particular brand; Laura watched while Dom Duarte flicked a lighter and held the flame to her cigarette. The two appeared to be looking into each other's eyes, and once again significant glances were exchanged between Pedro and his wife.

'You know,' remarked Rex very softly, 'those two could be seriously attracted to one another—in love, I mean.'

Laura turned to him, aware that Dom Duarte's eyes were now on her and not on the Portuguese girl.

'In love?' She shook her head. 'I don't believe that Dona Eduarda is capable of loving anyone.'

'You could be right, I suppose,' he conceded after a moment's thought. 'She has a hard face, I'll give you that.'

The evening wore on and it now seemed most unlikely that any announcement would be made. Laura found herself actually breathing a deep sigh of relief when at last the guests were ready to leave.

'Thank you for a lovely evening,' said Melanie. 'Laura, you must come to see us next week-end. It doesn't matter that Rex won't be here.'

Murmuring her thanks, Laura glanced at Rex, to see a disconsolate expression cross his face. However, he thanked the Conde graciously and a few minutes later Laura was saying goodnight to him in the hall.

'Dona Eduarda's not very partial to you, my girl,' stated Rex as he was leaving. His mouth was close to Laura's ear, and she caught the Conde's disapproving eye as he noticed this intimacy on Rex's part. 'She looks daggers at you most of the time.'

Although Laura was well aware that this was true, she merely laughed and said lightly,

'Your imagination's running away with you, Rex!'

He shrugged his shoulders, bade her goodnight, and went down the white marble steps in the wake of his sister and brother-in-law.

CHAPTER EIGHT

On the following Monday morning Laura was in the Gallery when Dom Duarte came up, a certain casualness about him that to Laura was both new and attractive. Again she told herself that he was human, and again she found the question hovering on the edge of her mind: had anyone ever progressed to the point of intimacy with this illustrious nobleman whose domain was nothing less than the entire island, this in addition to the vast pastures and vineyards and cork forests he owned in his native Portugal?

His presence here in the Gallery was disconcerting, to say the least; his voice, though, was quiet and friendly as he inquired how the work was going on.

'I've been carrying out several tests as to colours,' Laura explained, disturbed by his nearness, by the faint elusive smell of body lotion, fresh as the breeze drifting down from the pine-clad mountains. This stirring of her emotions, this new and exciting sensation which circled between her heart and mind, this awareness of the admission she had been forced to make ... all these spelled love ... Love! And for a man as distant as the stars! A man exalted, a nobleman whose looks and physique and personality were superlative. Fool that she was! Rex, now, was well within her reach, so why hadn't she shown her innate common sense and responded to the man who was on her own level?

'Your tests have proved successful?' the Conde was asking.

'Some of them; others have not.' She went on to explain some technical details, doubting whether his interest would be held, but it was. He wanted to know everything that was going on. This interest never flagged and each morning he would come up and talk with her for a few minutes. She began to wonder if he had doubts about her ability to restore these two paintings, and in consequence he was watching closely her progress. However, he never spoke one word of criticism, but rather did he now and then give her a word of praise. As usual she would colour as embarrassment took possession of her. Dom Duarte's eyes would sometimes darken with the most odd expression and on these particular occasions he would invariably become curt and cold with her, just as if he were remembering the social barrier that existed between them.

As for Laura herself, she was enjoying the work immensely, confident of success. She and Rex had said goodbye but he was intending to write to her quite often, he said. He would be back on the island at Christmas time and hoped she would still be here. Well, that all depended on the Conde, and whether he would permit her to work on those paintings which she had originally come here to restore.

'*Senhorita*,' he said one day, 'I asked you for those testimonials.'

'Oh . . .' She had completely forgotten to give them to him, so absorbed had she been in her work. 'I'll bring them to you after lunch.'

'Good. I shall be in my study for the whole of the afternoon.' His eyes wandered to the picture she was working on, giving it the final touching up. She stood back so that his view was not blocked, saw him nod his head in a satisfied way, and felt exultant.

'Excellent,' he observed. 'And the other?'

'It's ready for the final touching up—when this blue is dry, that is.'

'You have great talent,' he said, and Laura knew that such an admission from the Conde was praise indeed. She coloured, thanked him shyly and then turned away, hiding her embarrassment.

The testimonials were delivered later in the day. The Conde, having invited her to enter his study, merely accepted the envelope from her and said coolly,

'Thank you; I shall read them and let you have them back this evening.'

Suave, dispassionate. A man of many moods, decided Laura, remembering how human he could be at times.

The following morning she was riding Nayrilla in the Great Park when she sensed another presence. She turned her head, and saw the Conde sitting on a fallen tree, his horse tethered to another tree a short distance away.

'*Senhorita*,' he murmured, and she saw the glint of a smile touch his lips. 'You're not with Clara and her nanny this morning?' He looked questioningly at her; she dismounted, driven to this action by a compulsion she could not resist.

'They're not ready yet,' she said, aware that her hair had been flying behind her and must be untidy. Almost nervously she fumbled with it, endeavouring to put it to rights. 'I'm early, but you, Dom Duarte, must have been very early indeed.' Laura thought of Dona Eduarda, who usually rode with the Conde, and wondered if she, like Clara and Marianna, was still in bed.

'The sun was too tempting by far,' said Dom Duarte, his cool gaze fixed upon Laura's flushed face. 'Do you usually rise so early, *senhorita*?'

'Not this early,' she answered with a laugh. 'At home we don't have the sun to waken us at so early an hour.'

His gaze was still fixed upon her, in a sort of searching scrutiny. And there was a hint of indecision about him which puzzled her. This, she decided, was one of his 'human' moods. Yes, indeed, because he was smiling at her, and there was a strange softness about his face, as if some of the stern lines had been miraculously erased.

'Sit down,' he invited, indicating the tree trunk. 'You'll find the seat a little hard, but not too uncomfortable, for all that.'

Shyly she obeyed, choosing a spot some distance from where he himself sat. Her heart was fluttering; she was by no means sure she wanted to stay with him ... yet she did not want to go ...

'For some time now I have been thinking, *senhorita*, of that incident when Clara went into the sea,' began the Conde unexpectedly. 'I suggest you tell me exactly what happened——?'

'Tell you what happened?' she repeated, startled, and forgetting his strictures about interrupting him.

'Yes!' returned the Conde briefly.

Laura stared straight ahead, searching her mind for an answer. That the Conde suspected that all was not as it had appeared was evident, but just what would be his reaction if she told him the whole truth? Laura would clear herself, and there was nothing she would like better, naturally, but what of Clara? It seemed to Laura—knowing the Conde as she did—that he would consider untruths in an even graver light than the wilful damage done to his paintings. He would punish the child severely ... No, Laura could not tell him the truth, she decided firmly. She herself would have to lie, that was all.

'You know what happened, Dom Duarte,' she replied in low respectful tones. 'I invited Clara to come into——' His raised hand halted her words. He said imperiously,

'I repeat, Miss Conroy, I want you to tell me exactly what happened that day.'

She coloured instantly, disconcerted by his awareness of what she intended doing.

'Does it—it matter?' she murmured after a pause.

The grey eyes were fixed speculatively on her profile.

'It would seem that I must give you an order, Miss Conroy.'

She turned her head.

'An order?'

The Conde's mouth compressed.

'I want to know the truth!' he snapped. 'Immediately!'

She bit her lip. No use prevaricating any longer, and yet ...

'Dom Duarte, will you please make me a promise?' The words were out before she realised just how he would take them. 'Clara——'

'Miss Conroy,' he said icily, 'people do not attempt to bargain with me!'

'No ... I'm sorry——'

'The truth, now!'

Admitting that she had no alternative than to tell him what had happened, Laura began to speak, watching his face becoming grimmer and grimmer. She hesitated a moment, then decided that she ought not to divulge the lie which Dona Eduarda had told. The Conde was in all probability intending to marry the girl, and it seemed to Laura that he would be shocked at the idea of Dona Eduarda's unnecessary lie, and in consequence he would be unhappy. No, decided Laura firmly, she must not give the girl away.

'Well?' asked Dom Duarte softly as Laura continued to hesitate.

'That's all,' she shrugged, hoping he would not suspect that she had kept a part of it from him.

The grey eyes stared into hers, subjecting them to a most searching scrutiny. At length he said, still in the same soft tone,

'You're sure, Miss Conroy, that you have told me everything?'

She swallowed. It was so difficult to lie while he was staring at her in this direct manner. However, she did at least manage to say, with reasonable conviction, that there was nothing else to tell him. He continued to look at her as if he was not quite sure. And then, to her great relief, he nodded in acceptance of what she had said. But his face was stern and she now realised that the part she herself had played was to bring down his wrath upon her head. After his homily was over he added,

'So along with the lie told by Clara, you yourself lied?' The censure in his voice matched the expression in his eyes. 'Lied again by your silence.'

Laura hung her head, unable to meet his gaze.

'I s-suppose it w-was like lying,' she murmured contritely. 'But at the same time I could see no gain in getting Clara into trouble.' A silence followed, and eventually she lifted her face and looked at him. 'Can't you see, Dom Duarte, just how difficult it was for me?' The sincerity in his voice was bound to affect him, and she saw his face soften slightly. Again he nodded, thoughtfully. Laura knew for sure that he was now understanding her position at that time.

'I do see that there was some excuse,' he conceded at last, but went on to add that he was nonetheless disgusted, both with Laura and with his niece. Relieved that his real anger had subsided, Laura ventured to ask,

'Please don't punish Clara, will you?'

The Conde's face was coldly arrogant.

'Miss Conroy,' he said through tightly-compressed lips, 'I shall deal with my niece as I think, considering her deceit, and the fact that she is in my charge and, therefore, must be punished for any misdemeanours.'

Laura frowned, and noticed his cold eyes narrow.

'*Senhor*,' she begged, undaunted by his austerity, 'can you not see the situation from the child's point of view? You now know—because I have just explained to you —the reason why Clara damaged the paintings. In her child's mind this was making amends because, as I said, she had guessed that the lie she had told had caused you to send me away.' Laura paused, to note the Conde's reaction. His face was a mask, cold and unreadable. 'She's only five, Dom Duarte,' she added on a little desperate note. 'There's no real wickedness in her.'

No answer from the Conde. He was watching his horse, Burkan, contentedly cropping grass growing beneath the tree to which he was tethered. His face was thoughtful; Laura had the impression that he was weighing her words, willing to consider them seriously, and to draw a final conclusion. She waited a little breathlessly for his voice to break the silence, which at length it did. He had turned to her again, his interest appearing to have been arrested in some inexplicable way.

'Perhaps I shall be lenient with Clara,' he said, but this was by no means a firm promise. 'You appear to have an understanding of a child's mind, Miss Conroy?'

'Is isn't because I've had much to do with children,' she admitted. 'I expect every woman has a certain amount of instinct regarding them.' She spoke matter-of-factly, not realising that the Conde might be weighing these words too, and deciding there was a great deal of common sense in them. His cool and alien voice had a strange ring to it as he said,

'You'll make a very understanding mother, one day.'

She coloured, naturally, and glanced away, to where her own horse was standing, his coat gleaming in the sunshine.

'It's nice of you to say so, *senhor*,' she murmured after a while. But she added, this time with a wry grimace, 'Perhaps I shall never marry, though, for I'm exceedingly fond of my work.'

Her companion responded by saying that, in England, many married women continued to follow their chosen careers, at least, for a time.

'I have a friend in England whose wife manages to work as a secretary and yet bring up a family. She has a nanny, of course.'

Surprised that he should have said this without a trace of contempt or disdain entering his voice, Laura said impulsively,

'You don't consider it wrong, then, for a married woman to follow her career?'

'In England it's accepted that she should.' For a second his eyes rested on her shining russet-brown hair and all she could think of was that it was wind-teased, so different from the immaculate elegance of Dona Eduarda's. 'In Portugal, and in Torassa, of course, this would not be permitted—not in the Portuguese families, that is. The natives of the island do often have both husband and wife contributing to the expenses of the home.'

'A wife's place is in the house?' Laura knew there was a note of criticism in her voice and was not surprised to see the Conde's brows lift a fraction. 'In Portugal, I mean?'

'It is a woman's destiny to take care of the home,' he retorted evenly. 'The man is the breadwinner.'

'A rather antiquated idea, is it not?'

'In your country, yes,' he replied. 'In my country, no.'

Laura shrugged her shoulders. She was suddenly thinking of his words about her making a good mother ... and she knew again the deep attraction of the Conde, was aware of the sort of hopeless pleasure of his company, now that his censure was past. She found herself picturing his children ... And hers ...

A smile leapt involuntarily to her face, and with it that moist and limpid quality to her eyes. The Conde's attention became focused on the charming picture she made, sitting there, some small distance from him, against a background of exotic vegetation and thickly-foliaged trees. The tropical sun burnished her hair, and highlighted the delicate lines of her face. Laura saw a muscle move in his throat, saw the withdrawal of his gaze, which he then concentrated on his horse. He was distant all at once, as if he had no interest in her at all. She had the odd and half-vague sensation that he was vexed with himself, that he was taking himself sternly in hand—as when one puts a rein on one's impulses because they are leading one astray. And to support this idea the Conde rose majestically from his seat, bowed stiffly as he bade her goodbye. Laura rose also but stood quite still, watching him swing lightly on to Burkan's back and ride along the path until, eventually, he and the horse were lost to view.

A deep sigh escaped her; she was fighting desperately to put from her thoughts of love, profoundly aware of her foolishness, and of the vast gulf which yawned between the Conde and herself. Even if by some miracle he were to fall in love with her, it would never serve, so great was the social distance between them. He, a wealthy Portuguese *fidalgo*, a man of the most noble birth; she, an ordinary English girl working for her living, a girl whose only assets—from the material point of view—were a flat and its contents.

'Not that he ever would fall in love with me,' she sighed, taking up the bridle and at the same time patting the gleaming neck of her horse. 'I don't believe he could fall in love with anyone; he's too austere, too coldly impersonal.' Emotions like deep affection and love were unknown to him, she felt sure. They would always be unknown to him, and therefore it was as well that his interest lay with a woman like Dona Eduarda who herself was cold and unemotional.

Exactly a week later Laura was in the Gallery, examining other paintings and making more detailed notes than those she had made previously. For the Conde, expressing himself more than satisfied with her work on the two which had been damaged by his niece, had not hesitated to ask her to restore the rest. He came up and turned with a swift smile. Dona Eduarda had left the Palacio that very morning, and for Laura it seemed that a shadow had been lifted from the house.

'How much progress have you made?' he asked.

'I'm doing all the preliminaries,' she told him. 'It's always difficult to define the colours exactly. I'm making notes on my own suggestions for the mixing of certain colours. Of course, the pictures must be washed first, as you know.'

The Conde nodded thoughtfully, putting out a finger to touch a brittle and discoloured patch on one of the paintings.

'It is obvious that this kind of work demands a great amount of concentration, *senhorita*. I feel you ought not to work such long hours as you have been doing.'

She looked swiftly at him, not quite sure if she had actually heard a note of concern in his voice, or if she had imagined it.

'I'm capable of working long hours——' she began, then stopped as she noticed the warning glint in his eye. It was an order he had given her, she realised, and he expected it to be obeyed without question. Nevertheless, she did make a small protest, saying she would take twice as long to do the work if she took the afternoons off, which was the impression she had from the way he spoke. 'There's such a lot of buckling——' She pointed, indicating one of the paintings which had suffered more than any of the others. 'It will be a long job, *senhor* ...' She tailed off, biting her lip.

'Not only do you interrupt me, *senhorita*,' said Dom Duarte coldly, 'but you argue with me as well.' The severity of his gaze brought the colour leaping to her cheeks, and at the same time caused her to lower her head, feeling guilty of some serious breach of etiquette. 'It might interest you to know that you are the only person who has ever had the impertinence to argue with me.'

'I'm sorry, *senhor*.' Laura swallowed hard, and concentrated on the painting in front of her. As before, she felt the censure of all these faces looking out from the canvases—ancestors of the Conde, illustrious men and their high-born wives and children.

'You will please me by working during the mornings only,' said the Conde in his cool accented voice. 'The afternoons will be your own.'

She nodded, her thoughts wildly unhappy despite the stern austerity with which she was being treated by her employer. Mornings only! This meant that the work would be prolonged, taking about a year. Yet rising as a barrier to her happiness was the acute realisation of her own feelings towards the Conde. To be near him, to have him come up here regularly to see what she was doing, to dine with him by candlelight ... How could she hide her love for a whole year? Better by far to stop now, and leave the Palacio. The next twelve months would then serve to make her forget ... but to go on would only mean that her love was kept vitally alive, and even be strengthened. Yes, that was inevitable, and yet she knew that common sense could never prevail, that it was the desire of her heart which she would follow. The Conde was eyeing her rather sternly, as if expecting her to make some further protest. She remained silent, a half-smile fluttering to her lips. The Conde's full attention became fixed on her eyes. He frowned, as though at his own thoughts, and turned away with an abruptness that startled her.

She watched him stroll around the Gallery, saw him stop now and then and study something that had caught his attention. He spoke, drawing her own attention to some flaw he had just discovered, asking if she herself had noticed.

Laura nodded at once.

'Yes, Dom Duarte. I rather think I have discovered just about everything.'

He gave a small sigh.

'It was little less than a tragedy that these lovely paintings were damaged.' His mouth tightened. 'The unreliability of workmen,' he added tersely. Laura was recalling how little faith he had had in her ability at first, and decided she could not altogether blame him.

'It certainly was a pity that you didn't know where the paintings would be stored.' He nodded absently. Laura had already mentioned that she knew how the paintings came to be damaged.

'One does not expect such stupidity,' he said after a space. He had turned towards her, but was now some distance from her. His eyes, though, were focused on her, and Laura found the colour mounting her cheeks. His interest was puzzling, and disconcerting too. She said, more to ease the moment than for any other reason,

'My father would have loved to work on these paintings.'

The Conde did not speak for a while. He appeared to be giving some consideration to what she had said.

'You would have accompanied him, though?' he commented at last. 'He always had you to assist him, you said?'

'Yes, that's right.' Was it imagination, or had the Conde been seeing a situation where she herself was absent, and her father working here, on his pictures? For one absurd moment Laura had the impression that Dom Duarte would have been sorry if her father had come here without her!

Her heart began to flutter; she protested inwardly at her foolishness in assuming, for one second, that the illustrious Conde Duarte André Volante de Taviro Mauredo could be *glad* that he had met her!

His attention had returned to one of the paintings. She automatically moved closer to him, and together they discussed what was to be done by way of restoration.

'I feel I am most fortunate in having you do this work for me,' stated the Conde unexpectedly, and on that he turned and strode swiftly from the room.

Strange man! Laura would have expected a smile to accompany words such as he had just uttered, but instead she felt sure he was frowning inwardly. And the abrupt termination of those words, then his hasty departure from her presence, almost as if he had to escape from something dangerous!

'Oh, dear, I'm all at sixes and sevens with him,' she sighed, addressing the obese and grotesque figure of the Conde's ancestor: Ricardo Soeiro José de Taviro Mauredo. 'He's distant and reserved one moment, but the next moment he's offering praise. Sometimes he's arrogant, letting me see that he's a man of importance, lord of Torassa. At other times he thaws out for a space but retains that air of superiority. He looks at me now and then as if he's found something interesting about my features, but suddenly he becomes aloof again, as if he considers he's lowering his dignity by this interest.' Laura grimaced at the whiskered face and moved away, to where she had been working when interrupted by the Conde.

That evening she and he dined alone. There was music to add further romance to the atmosphere and Laura found herself in a world of unreality, her mind a little dazed by the very idea of her being here at all, in this stately Palacio, dining by candlelight with its noble owner. He was immaculately attired, with that air of the aristocrat very much in evidence. So correct his every action! And yet so gracious too, as he inquired if she had enjoyed her meal.

'Yes, it was delicious.' She felt shy, but a smile came swiftly to her lips. Her eyes met his, moist and limpid. The Conde's mouth moved; she expected him to say something, but to her surprise he remained silent, speaking only after they had left the table and entered the sitting-room where Gigo was ready to serve them with their coffee and liqueurs. 'I expect you will be doing a little more exploring of our island, now that you're to work mornings only,' he said when they were both seated.

'I shall certainly try,' replied Laura, settling back in her big armchair. Her long dress of lilac-coloured lace trailed the floor, so full and flowing was its skirt. The bodice, high-waisted and with a mandarin collar, was very tight-fitting, so that her tender curves were more obvious than usual. Dom Duarte glanced her over; she had the impression that he would have liked his eyes to linger but that he was disciplining himself to remain indifferent and aloof.

'Teresa's available if you want her,' he said, picking up his glass. 'She knows Torassa from end to end.'

'Her people have always lived here?'

The Conde nodded.

'They're a most respected family. Her father and two brothers grow citrus fruits on their estate.'

'Estate?' Laura's eyes widened. 'People can have estates here, then?'

At her surprise he smiled faintly.

'I have an idea that you have branded me a feudal lord,' he said, watching for her reaction. She was nodding almost before he had finished speaking. 'I assure you, *senhorita*, that it isn't like that at all.'

'But you are the owner of this island.'

'Of course, and in consequence my word is law—which is as it should be. However, my tenants have rights, which is also as it should be. They use their lands as they wish, and I would object only if they should want to do something that would detract from the beauty, and the privacy, of our island.'

Laura looked at him, noting that he referred to Torassa as 'our' island, which in effect meant that he regarded it in the light of the heritage of the natives just as much as his own heritage.

'It's wonderful that you can keep the island so private,' she said at length.

'I shall always endeavour to keep it private, not only for myself, but for those who, like me, want to avoid any form of commercialism.'

'The natives want to keep it to themselves, obviously.'

'I believe that, if anyone else had bought it from the Englishman, it would have been a holiday resort by now. So many people are concerned with money. They despoil nature's wonderful work in order to possess far more money than they require.'

She thought about this and found it to be true. However, she knew that the Conde had so much wealth he would never be able to use any extra money and therefore it was reasonable to assume that the total absence of necessity had at least something to do with his attitude regarding the island's destiny. She could not resist asking,

'Would you feel the same, Dom Duarte, if you were less wealthy than you are?' and it was only when the question was out that she realised just how impertinent it must sound. He seemed not to have noticed, because as she looked at him over the rim of her glass she saw that he was considering her words.

'Yes,' he answered presently, 'I would feel the same. To be comfortable is the most important factor of living, Mis Conroy. What is the use of a great deal of money if one is surrounded by masses of flats and supermarkets, by hideous artificial lights which mask the stars and the moon? What good is a white-sanded shore if instead of it being fringed with palm trees it has ugly ice-cream stalls and is littered with orange peel and toffee papers?'

'You know all about these things?' she said in surprise.

144

The Conde's straight dark brows lifted a fraction.

'I do travel,' he returned haughtily. 'I also have a home in Lisbon.'

Laura coloured slightly.

'I meant the toffee papers, and the ice-cream stalls,' she murmured, staring into her glass rather than at the Conde.

'Those one does see in Lisbon, Miss Conroy.'

'I expect,' she said, 'that you visit this other home only when it is necessary?'

'Quite right.' The Conde picked up his coffee and took a drink. 'Torassa was bought so that my people could have a home in natural surroundings. We have all treasured it, being grateful indeed to the man who purchased it.'

Laura suddenly recalled Avice's saying that men like the Conde never stop to think that it was their ancestors whom they had to thank for what they possessed. It was not like that with Dom Duarte, obviously; he was more than grateful for his inheritance. Laura warmed to him, glad that she was able to find attractive traits to his nature. The recollection of what Avice had said naturally brought with it other things which she and Laura had mentioned, as, for instance, the Conde's austere wife, and his sons. A swift and irrepressible smile leapt to her lips, and her eyes shone with amusement. The Conde, noticing her change of expression, looked askance at her and, when she offered him no explanation of her humour he asked outright,

'What is it that you find so amusing, *senhorita*?'

Instinctively she shook her head, to indicate her inability to explain. But his concentrated gaze was compelling, even coercive, and Laura found herself saying,

'It was something my friend and I were discussing the evening before I came here.'

'Yes?'

'I—er—we concluded you'd be married, with several grown-up sons.'

The dark brows shot up.

'Indeed? And what, might I ask, gave you an idea like that?'

'I really don't know,' she admitted. 'We both took it for granted that you would be much older than you are.'

'And with a wife ...' The Conde spoke softly, to himself, but his eyes were fixed on Laura's face, the most odd expression in their depths. 'Tell me, *senhorita*, what was my wife like?'

Laura looked at him in surprise, having expected him to be annoyed on hearing of the conclusions which she and Avice had come to.

'She too was older, naturally,' she replied presently, and with some hesitation.

The Conde said perceptively,

'And not a very nice person, eh?'

'Oh ... er ... we never thought of her like that——' Dom Duarte's imperious gesture brought her protest to an abrupt stop.

'I have my own ideas as to the picture which you conjured up,' he said, not without a hint of amusement which added to her surprise. 'However, I shall not embarrass you by insisting you confess all.' A smile curved his lips and Laura caught her breath. He was too attractive by far! Every nerve and sense was affected by this attraction. She felt excitement and hopelessness mingling with fear—fear that she would never really recover from the hurt which would be hers when eventually she had to leave the island, never to set eyes upon Dom Duarte again. Her eyes shadowed and he noticed. His own eyes flickered strangely and he seemed to frown.

She sensed a certain hesitancy about him, a struggle of some kind going on in his mind. She heard a soft sigh escape him, felt it was half impatient, half angry.

And suddenly it was imperative that she get away, for the whole atmosphere seemed charged with tension.

'I think I'll go for my usual stroll,' she said, drinking the last of her coffee. 'If you will excuse me, Dom Duarte?'

To her surprise he frowned and said, glancing at the clock,

'It's early yet, *senhorita*. Perhaps you would like to listen to some records?'

She shook her head instinctively.

'I'd rather go out,' she said, staring at him. 'It's so beautiful out there, in the gardens.' She rose as she spoke, and moved uncertainly towards the door, afraid of offending him and yet unwilling to stay, because of the way she felt, and because of the Conde's strange attitude towards her, which was more friendly than it had ever been before. Laura had never expected any real show of friendliness from him owing to the fact that he believed that she had intended leaving his niece to drown.

'Very well, *senhorita*.' His voice was cool, impersonal. 'You must do as you wish.'

She left the room, dejection sweeping over her at the change in his voice and manner. Yet she had only herself to blame; she could have stayed, and chatted to him.

'Why didn't I?' she asked herself angrily as she wandered in the gardens a few moments later. 'Why didn't I stay with him, enjoying his company? He wanted me to—he must have done so, for otherwise he wouldn't have asked me to stay.'

CHAPTER NINE

IT was a week later that Marianna complained of a sore throat, but when the Conde suggested she stay in bed she assured him that she could carry on with her duties. However, noticing the girl's pallor and listlessness, Dom Duarte ordered her to take a rest.

'Will Teresa take charge of Clara?' Laura inquired, but the Conde shook his head, informing her that he had given Teresa a week's leave in order that she could spend some time in the house which she and Martin were renovating.

'I wonder,' continued Dom Duarte, 'if you yourself would look after Clara for a while?'

Laura stared, surprised that he would trust her to take good care of the child, believing as he did that she had left Clara to drown. He was looking inquiringly at her and she said she would be happy to take on the role of nanny to his niece. He then went on to warn Laura that she was a handful, and that if Laura did take on the responsibility he was asking of her, he would expect her to keep the child out of mischief.

'I'll take good care of her,' promised Laura.

'If you do have trouble with her then you must come to me immediately.'

Laura nodded, although she did not contemplate any trouble with Clara, since she and the child had always got along excellently together.

'Being with you will improve her English,' the Conde stated. 'Marianna tends to speak in Portuguese for much of the time—when she and Clara are alone, that is.'

Clara was delighted at the idea of being with Laura. They rode together, and went for long walks into the woods or along the seashore, where they collected numerous shells and pieces of coral. These Laura decided to make into a sort of collage. Dom Duarte saw this in progress and commented on Laura's flair for the artistic.

'It's natural,' she smiled. 'I've been brought up in the world of art.'

'Perhaps,' he suggested, 'you would allow Clara to try her hand with this collage?'

'Of course. In fact, she has already glued on some of the shells and coral.'

'You're not afraid of her spoiling it, obviously?'

'She'll not be perfect, but it doesn't matter. Children love to be creative and they never see anything wrong with their own work, not at Clara's age, that is.' Laura paused, expecting the Conde to make some remark, but when he remained silent she continued, 'One should not, of course, bring the child's attention to any faults which he or she has made. Not at first. Too much fault-finding only discourages children and they lose interest.'

'You have a rather wonderful philosophy where the minds of children are concerned.' Dom Duarte's voice was soft, gentle almost, and in his eyes there was a warmth she had never encountered before. 'As I once remarked, you will make an excellent mother one day.'

Laura inclined her head so that her expression was hidden from those shrewd grey eyes of his. The last thing she wanted him to know was that his manner disturbed her, that his praise brought swift colour to her cheeks ... that her lips were moving tremulously, the result of the increased speed of her heartbeats. She considered his words, wondering if she ever would be a mother, now that she had given her heart to this man who was so far above her, so totally out of reach emotionally. Perhaps, a long time hence, she would find that the threads of her memory had weakened, that the Conde's face was no longer clearly etched in her mind. She might meet someone whom she could marry ... A great wave of dejection swept over her, and found outlet in a trembling sigh. The Conde spoke, asking in some concern if anything was wrong.

'No,' she answered at once. 'No, Dom Duarte.'

'Look at me.' So soft the command, but imperious for all that. Laura nevertheless ignored it and heard the Conde repeat it, even more softly, yet this time she was impelled to obey him.

She lifted her face, her eyes meeting his intense and searching scrutiny.

'You are upset about something,' he asserted. 'What is it?'

'Nothing, *senhor*.'

'*Senhorita*,' he said sternly, 'you do not always tell me the truth.'

She stared at him, catching her breath. For there was a subtle implication in his tone which made her wonder—as she had already wondered—if he had doubts as to the truth of Dona Eduarda's accusation that Laura intended leaving Clara to her own fate. Was he saying—though not in actual words—that she, Laura, had lied even yet again, by her silence? She said, playing for time,

'I don't understand you, Dom Duarte.'

The steely grey eyes glinted, still watching her face intently.

'I believe you do understand, *senhorita*. Yes, I believe you understand much.' And on that very cryptic statement the Conde turned on his heel and left her, without any further pursuance of the question which he had seemed so intent on her answering.

That afternoon Laura and Clara went walking into the hills. The ground in parts was marshy where pockets of peat had formed. Clara suddenly decided to run through one of these marshy areas and to Laura's horror she began to sink swiftly into the sodden peat.

'Clara!' she cried, fear rising as she saw the child's feet and ankles disappear. 'Come out!' But Laura knew the futility of the order and without hesitation she herself entered the bog. The water squelched about her feet and legs, soon reaching her knees. Terror caught at her throat so that the cries she made could scarcely be heard, especially as Clara was herself screaming with terror. Her arms were raised, threshing at the air; she was almost up to her neck, and still sinking. 'Clara, give me your hand!' Laura was almost sobbing, her mind dazed by what had happened, and so swiftly that she scarcely had time to think of what she could do. 'Don't struggle—oh, please don't! You'll only sink further in!'

Despair swept over her like a deluge, since she herself was over waist-deep in the peat. And then, just as she reached the child and took hold of her hand, she heard the Conde's voice, urgent, stern, imperious. She stood still as ordered, while the Conde came to her, treading carefully so as not to make too great a disturbance of the boggy substance through which he was proceeding.

'Can you stay?' he asked abruptly.

'Yes—oh, yes! Clara's almost——'

'I'll take Clara and then come back for you. But stand still! If you move you'll sink far more quickly than if you do as you're told!' As he spoke he was lifting the screaming child from the mire, but his eyes were on Laura and she had no doubts at all that he was profoundly anxious about her. She heard his almost harsh voice commanding Clara to be quiet, saw him place her roughly on the firm ground and turn with haste to come back to Laura. He lifted her; she felt his heart throbbing almost wildly and was staggered by the fact that his emotions could be stirred in this way. It was of course quite natural that he would be troubled about her, but this seemed out of all proportion, especially as he was telling her that she would not have sunk to any dangerous depth, not after she had obeyed his order to stand still. She was crying softly when at last he placed her on the firm ground beside his niece.

'I'm sorry, *senhor*,' Laura apologised for crying. 'I was so afraid.'

'Of course you were.' So soft and compassionate, so gentle and understanding. Not so with Clara, who received a look that warned her of trouble to come, once he had her back at the Palacio. 'It was most fortunate that I happened to hear Clara's screams——' He sent her another dark and threatening glance which caused Laura to shiver. He was so very formidable in this mood! She said, unconsciously speaking her thoughts aloud,

'She's been punished enough, by the fright she's had.'

Dom Duarte said nothing, merely indicating the path from which Clara had run on deciding to explore the ground beyond. Laura, drenched to the waist, looked down grimly at her ruined slacks and shoes. Still, she and Clara were safe, and that was all that mattered. How the Conde came to be here at so opportune a moment she could not imagine, but learned later that he himself had decided to take a long walk, and by some miracle had chosen the route taken by Laura and her young charge.

Clara walked so slowly that her uncle had to tell her

to hurry, indicating that she should go in front as the path was narrow.

'I'm frightened of you,' she said in English, her glance going to Laura as if begging her to speak on her behalf. Laura could find nothing to say; in any case, she was wise enough to realise that the Conde would very soon put her in her place should she try to influence him as to the punishment which Clara would receive. Laura herself would have done very little other than telling Clara off, because, as she had said, the child had had such a fright that she would never be so venturesome again.

'I'm afraid,' said the Conde sternly, 'that you'll be even more afraid of me if you don't learn to behave.' He turned to Laura, who was walking at his side. 'I don't blame you at all for what has happened, Miss Conroy,' he assured her. 'I couldn't expect you to keep hold of her hand all the time.'

Laura said nothing, but was inwardly thankful that he had not blamed her. On their arrival at the Palacio Dom Duarte waived Laura's offer to see the child. He would get one of the maids to give her a bath and a change of clothes.

'You yourself are obviously most uncomfortable,' he observed, his eyes flickering over her. 'We must do something about compensating you for those clothes.'

She shook her head in protest.

'It doesn't matter, Dom Duarte,' she told him quietly. 'You saved us, and that's all that matters.' A smile touched her lips; the Conde seemed fascinated by the limpid quality of her eyes. His smile came, bringing her warmth, and a strange feeling of happiness. He was different, somehow, despite the sternness which lurked beneath the surface.

'Go and change,' he said when she would have spoken again. 'And take the rest of the day off.'

She did not argue, aware that it would be futile. Nor did she try to put in a word for Clara, once again sure that the Conde would tolerate no interference as regards his dealings with his niece.

About a week later Laura was given a large cardboard box by Teresa.

'From Dom Duarte,' she said with a bright smile. 'You are becoming a favourite with him, *senhorita*.'

'A—favourite?' repeated Laura, her pulse quickening. 'What do you mean, Teresa?' Laura's eyes were on the box which Teresa had thrust into her hands. The name of a fashion shop was on the lid; Laura remembered seeing the shop in the small town in which the teashop was situated.

'He smiled when he told me to give it to you. Dom Duarte does not smile very much, but you must have noticed this?'

'Yes.' Laura put the box on the bed, her mind bewildered as she tried to guess what it could contain. 'Er—thank you, Teresa.'

The dismissal was received with an affable inclination of Teresa's head and the next moment Laura was alone, her fascinated gaze fixed on the cardboard box. Slowly she untied the string, then lifted off the lid. A pair of slacks! Expensively-cut, she noticed as she lifted them from their wrapping of white tissue-paper. Underneath was a white sweater—almost identical to the one she had been wearing on the day she had gone into the bog after Clara. And beneath this, in a separate wrapping, was a pair of shoes to match the slacks.

'A complete outfit to replace the other ...' She could not accept it, of course. The very presence of it on her bed embarrassed her, and after only the merest hesitation she left her room and went down to find the

154

Conde. He was in the garden, strolling along the edge of the lake, idly watching the waterfowl swimming about in the tropical sunshine. Many trees were in flower and their perfume wafted across to where Laura was walking, taking a short cut across a wide velvet lawn fringed with delicate almond trees and exotic flowers grouped according to their various colours, creating a delightful mosaic when viewed from a distance.

The Conde turned his head and then stopped, a smile coming slowly to his lips. The inquiry in his eyes faded the moment Laura began to speak, when presently she reached him.

'Dom Duarte, it is kind of you to replace the things I spoiled, but I cannot accept your gift.' The words came all of a rush, as the Conde's expression was changing to one of near arrogance. 'It wouldn't be right,' she added before he could speak.

'No? Why not?'

'Well ... clothes ...'

The arrogance was dispelled unexpectedly, to be replaced by a hint of amusement.

'There would be no objection if, for example, you had ruined something less personal?'

Laura coloured slightly.

'I suppose you are right,' she admitted after a pause.

'It is my wish, *senhorita*, that you accept the replacements.'

She shook her head automatically, and avoided his gaze by concentrating on a humming-bird that hovered above a vivid crimson anthurium flower.

'The slacks I spoiled were far from new, *senhor*,' she said at last.

'I fail to see what that has got to do with it,' was Dom Duarte's cool rejoinder. 'As I have said, it is my wish that you accept the replacements.'

She looked at him, frowning.

'Surely I can refuse them, Dom Duarte?'

'No, *senhorita*, you can't.'

Laura blinked at him, pretending not to have heard the imperious note in his voice.

'The sweater wasn't ruined, not altogether.'

To her surprise the Conde actually laughed. She caught her breath, intensely conscious of his charm.

'Just half ruined, eh? The lower half, if I remember rightly.'

Her lip quivered, his amusement being infectious.

'I did go in up to my waist, I must admit,' she said, feeling rather foolish.

'The shoes fitted all right?' he asked.

'I haven't tried them on, naturally.'

'Teresa gave me the size; she also took the size of the other things.'

'Did she buy them?' asked Laura with a curious glance.

The Conde shook his head, informing her that his housekeeper had actually done the shopping for him. He was so calm about it all, just as if the buying of clothes for one of his employees was an everyday occurrence.

'I believe she did try to get the exact colour of the slacks and sweater but failed to do so. I trust the colours she did get are to your liking?'

Laura bit her lip, wondering how she was to make her protest take effect. But on seeing the sudden change in Dom Duarte's expression, she decided not to make any further protest at all. Instead she thanked him uneasily, stammering over her words. He listened in some amusement, his grey eyes almost twinkling. It was plain that her submissive attitude had served to please and satisfy him.

'Well, now that you've got that off your mind perhaps we can talk about something else?'

'Something else?' echoed Laura. 'I don't understand.'

The Conde gave her a curious look.

'The pictures,' he said after a slight pause. 'Tell me how they are getting along?'

'I haven't done very well this past week,' she answered. 'I was looking after Clara——'

'Yes, of course. But these last couple of days you've been working—during the mornings, that is.' He paused again and smiled at her reassuringly. 'I don't expect marvels, *senhorita*, as I have already given you to understand. If you are happy with the way the renovations are progressing, then I am also.'

'I'm perfectly satisfied,' she told him, returning his smile and at the same time endeavouring to ignore the fact that her emotions were being overwhelmingly affected by his presence in this most romantic setting of gardens and lake, of gay birds flitting about among the trees, and the tropical sunshine caressing the exotic, perfumed flowers which abounded everywhere. The marble statues gleamed white in the sun's rays; the fountain made a rainbow of colour before cascading down into the lake. 'I love the work,' added Laura enthusiastically. 'I do thank you, Dom Duarte, for letting me stay.'

He looked down into her face; Laura wished she could understand his expression, but it was unreadable. She swallowed hard, aware that her every nerve was affected, becoming tensed. It was a profound and intimate moment ... the sort of breathless interlude which precedes a first kiss. Startled by this incredible idea, Laura felt the hot colour flood her cheeks. She turned swiftly from him, intending to move away, but he seemed to guess at her intention and his hand shot out, catching her by the wrist. That it was an involuntary action was evident by the amazement that leapt into his eyes. He seemed staggered that he had forgotten his dignity to this extent. And yet he made no move to release her, and they both stood and staring down, at his hand holding her wrist.

'I—I—th-think I had better be going,' she stammered at last.

'Yes.' The Conde's voice was edged with a sort of anger; she wondered at the reason for it and glanced up. His face was expressionless. But suddenly he smiled, as if he had forgotten the tinge of anger that assailed him. 'I would prefer that you stay a while,' he said, and she stared incredulously at him.

'Stay?'

'I find I desire company.'

'But—er ...'

'Yes?'

'Surely, *senhor*, you don't desire *my* company?'

The Conde let go of her wrist.

'What makes you think that I don't desire your company, *senhorita*?'

She shook her head in bewilderment.

'There seems no reason why you should,' she returned reasonably.

At this Dom Duarte's eyes flickered with amusement. How different he was today!

'If I were to say that I find pleasure in your company, would you then be less puzzled by my desire?'

'I don't—don't understand you, sir.' The last word escaped unbidden and she looked for a sign that she had vexed him. The smile still lingered in his eyes. 'I should be less puzzled, naturally, but I am only a servant, *senhor*.'

To her surprise this statement produced a swift frown.

'No such thing! I believe I said, right at the start, that I would never have looked upon your father as a servant. That applies to you, *senhorita*. You are doing a valuable service, but you are not a servant!'

She glanced away, hurt by the change in his manner.

'If you really want me to stay,' she began, 'then of course I shall be happy to do so.'

He actually laughed.

'So formal a little speech! *Senhorita*, I really do want you to stay.' His voice had softened; his gaze was definitely persuasive. Laura's heart seemed to turn a somersault and her eyes were like stars. The Conde appeared to be intensely aware of her, seemed to have thrown his dignity to the winds. 'Come, *senhorita*, let us walk in the Park.'

She fell into step beside him as he moved, continuing alongside the lake. Water-lilies floated in profusion, and brightly-coloured butterflies settled on them, then winged away to settle on some other flowers growing on the grassy bank.

'What an idyllic place this is!' exclaimed Laura, quite unable to contain her appreciation a moment longer. 'How privileged I am to be here!'

'And how privileged I am to have you, *senhorita*,' was the Conde's staggering admission. 'You thanked me just now for allowing you to stay. I believe I must thank you for agreeing to stay.'

Laura fell silent, unable to speak for the emotion which had her in its grip. Where was this kind of talk leading? That the Conde's manner and voice were totally different from anything she had experienced before was an undoubted fact. She might have been his friend ... a friend who could become more ...

The walk lasted over an hour; they chatted about the Palacio, about the paintings, about the island. But Laura eventually found herself being questioned about herself, her life in England, and her job. She answered his every query, wondering at his interest while at the same time conscious of his changed manner, of the unmistakable intimacy which had sprung up between them.

'So you live quite alone, in this flat you speak of?'

'Yes, that's right.'

'It must become monotonous at times?'

'Only when I'm not working.'

'You have periods when you don't work?'

'Sometimes there are no pictures to restore,' she explained. 'And then I'm idle, waiting for something to turn up. This doesn't happen very often, though.'

'I see ...' He became thoughtful and for a while they proceeded in silence, making for the Palacio, that stately *senhorial* mansion, its outline standing clearly visible above the shrubbery that marked the dividing line between the Great Park and the formal gardens that surrounded the house. 'So if you left England no one would miss you.' The words were spoken so softly that Laura only just caught them. But she did catch them, and her heart seemed to jerk from its moorings. She wanted to speak, to ask him what he meant, but she could not find the right words. The Conde spoke again, but this time she failed to catch even anything except the short phrase, 'not possible'.

Not possible ... What did that mean? She looked up, to find him deep in thought, to see that his fine lips were compressed, and that his jawline was flexed.

'*Senhorita*,' he was saying when eventually they neared the house, 'thank you very much for the most pleasant stroll.'

'Thank *you*, Dom Duarte,' she returned with a spontaneous smile. 'It was lovely!'

'Yes.' The brief word was spoken mechanically. 'Er—I'm afraid I shan't be dining at home this evening *senhorita*. So perhaps you will arrange for your dinner to be brought up to your room? See Teresa about it.'

'Yes, *senhor* ...' Her voice failed, because he was already walking away, and because she had, with sudden enlightenment, realised just what he meant when he uttered those two words,

'... not possible.'

CHAPTER TEN

THAT the Conde had come to regard her in a very different light from that of a girl who could do him a service by restoring his paintings was abundantly clear to Laura; that he had realised that a more intimate relationship was out of the question was also abundantly clear.

'He likes me—he knows he could love me, but the social gulf precludes marriage between us.' Tears filled Laura's eyes; absurdly she wished he would lose all his money, and even his position, and come down to her level.

'Dona Eduarda is coming to Torassa again,' Teresa was telling Laura a few days later. 'I wonder if they will become engaged to be married.'

Laura knew the colour was fading from her cheeks as she responded,

'Perhaps they will, Teresa. They—they are eminently suited to one another.'

'Well . . .' The girl hesitated, a slight frown creasing her high forehead. 'For me, *senhorita*, I prefer to be very much in love with my husband.' A happy smile accompanied Teresa's pronouncement and Laura gave a deep, dejected sigh. 'But for the Conde,' went on Teresa, 'it is necessary that he marries a lady of his own class, and, as you say, Dona Eduarda is therefore quite suitable as his wife.'

Laura, who had been working all the morning in the Gallery, went off into town to do some shopping. Marianna was fully recovered, and able to resume her duties as nanny to Clara, so Teresa was as usual there to attend to anything which Laura should require in the way of meals in her room, or the collection of her soiled linen, which she took to the Palacio laundry, and brought back later, beautifully washed and ironed. Dom Duarte had dined with Laura once only since that walk in the Park, inviting her to join him a couple of evenings ago. Laura would have liked to refuse, knowing just how the Conde felt about her, but she could find no excuse for doing so. In any case, she found herself actually looking forward to the interlude of exquisite pain which a few hours with the Conde would give her.

She wore the new outfit for her trip into town, finding pleasure in the wearing of such expensive clothes. Teresa had done her work well, as everything fitted to perfection.

'Laura!' The friendly voice of Melanie came to Laura as she stood looking in a shop window, and she turned eagerly, a swift smile of pleasure leaping to her lips. 'Hello! We haven't seen you for ages.' Melanie, attractively attired in a lightweight trouser suit, looked Laura over appreciatively. 'You haven't taken advantage of your open invitation. You could have come any time, you know that.'

'Yes, I know. As a matter of fact, I've been rather busy lately. Marianna was ill and I was looking after Clara for a few days. Then I began to explore the island, with Teresa at times, and by myself at others.'

Melanie nodded understandingly.

'Life's a rush on occasions, even here, on Torassa.'

'Well,' submitted Laura with all honesty, 'I haven't exactly been rushing around. I'm working mornings only at present, so have my afternoons free, and that's why I've been able to do some exploring.'

'Mornings only?' Melanie said in surprise. 'How is that?'

'Dom Duarte said I musn't work too hard.'

Melanie's eyebrows shot up.

'He did? Anxious about you, it would appear.'

Laura had thought so at the time he had told her she must cut down her hours. Now, however, she wondered if he were only being practical, on the assumption that she would obviously work better in the cooler part of the day, and at a time when she was fresh, and her mind alert after a night's sleep.

'Are you alone?' she inquired of Melanie, automatically glancing around to see if Pedro was anywhere about.

'Yes; Pedro never comes to town if he can help it.'

'It's a beautiful little town, though.' Laura had already decided it was the prettiest town she had ever seen, or ever would see. Over the main thoroughfare flowering trees met, and half way along this street was a picturesque bridge spanning a swiftly-flowing river, along the banks of which grew exotic flowers in a gay profusion of delightful colour.

'Yes, I agree,' returned Melanie. 'And it's quite surprising that one can buy almost anything one requires.' She glanced at Laura's outfit. 'Did you buy those here?'

Laura went red and turned away.

'They did come from one of these shops, I believe.'

Melanie stared in some bewilderment but tactfully refrained from asking questions. Relieved, Laura asked if Melanie had time to spare for afternoon tea.

'I always have time,' answered Melanie with a laugh. 'And it'll be nice to have company for a change.' There was an odd inflection in her voice as she added, 'I've been wanting to have a little talk with you, as a matter

164

of fact, and that's why I hoped you'd come along and see us.'

They entered the teashop and ordered tea and cakes. Laura waited for Melanie to speak, curious to know what she had to tell her.

'I had a letter from Rex last week,' began Melanie. 'He was wondering why you hadn't written in answer to his last letter.'

Laura coloured slightly. She had received three letters altogether from Rex, but had answered only two, since the third one was far more friendly than she liked. Rex in fact had written what could almost be termed a love-letter. And so she had put off answering it, not wanting to hurt his feelings while at the same time wondering how she could reply without injecting a coolness into her letter that would act as a rebuff and ensure his not writing in that particular vein again.

'I've been rather busy,' she answered lamely at last.

'He likes you a lot, Laura.' Melanie idly took up her serviette and shook it out before placing it on her knee. 'I've never known him show so much interest in a girl before.'

'I'm not intending to have a boy-friend just yet.'

'I see ...' Melanie looked at Laura across the table. 'He's a hard-working, decent young man, Laura.'

'I don't doubt that for one moment,' returned Laura swiftly. 'It's just that I myself am not ready to have a boy-friend.'

'Don't you want to get married, then?'

Laura thought of the Conde and those two words he had uttered, words that had meant so much, that had brought Laura down from the happy heights to which she had risen during the stroll they had had in the grounds of the Palacio. The Conde, she knew, had come very close to caring for her, but had pulled himself up in time, profoundly conscious of the difference in their positions. The noble Conde Duarte André Volante de Taviro Mauredo could never marry a penniless English girl without rank or background.

'I certainly don't want to marry yet—not for a long time, in fact.' Long time? Would she ever be able to fall in love again? wondered Laura, a terrible dejection engulfing her. She felt she would always be comparing any man she met with the Conde, and finding him sadly wanting. For the Conde was superlative among men and, having met and fallen in love with him, Laura could not for the life of her imagine any other man taking his place in her heart.

'Children,' murmured Melanie in a questioning tone, 'should come along fairly early in a woman's life.'

'I might never have children,' returned Laura in a resigned voice.

The tea and cakes arrived, much to Laura's relief. The conversation was not one she wanted to pursue. Melanie poured the tea, and the two girls chatted about the forthcoming marriage of Teresa and Martim, for a wedding on Torassa was always an event which interested everyone on the island. Later, they separated, Melanie to go to the market and Laura to the chemist and the small department store where she hoped to buy a present for Avice whose birthday was a fortnight hence.

'Do come and visit us,' pressed Melanie. 'We really do want you to come.'

'I will come,' promised Laura. 'Perhaps on Sunday afternoon.'

'We'll look forward to that,' smiled Melanie. 'Please don't disappoint us.' She went off, and Laura made her way along the street to the chemist's shop, her thoughts on what Melanie had said about Rex. Laura had already told herself that Rex was within her reach; she knew he would be a faithful and reliable husband.

'But not for me,' she whispered brokenly. 'I'm sure I'll never forget Dom Duarte sufficiently to marry anyone else.'

Dona Eduarda was dining with the Conde. Laura had not been invited to join them and she sat on the balcony of her room and ate the meal which Teresa had brought up for her. She was undecided about staying on to finish all the paintings. Those which she had already started must be finished, of course, but she felt she would not touch any of the others. Far wiser to leave as soon as was possible. She thought of what Teresa had said about the two becoming engaged, and pictured herself being here at the time when they were married. It was unthinkable! Laura felt she would not be able to bear it when, after the honeymoon, they returned to the Palacio and Dona Eduarda took up her position as mistress of the delightful establishment. Moreover, as the Portuguese girl so disliked Laura, it was reasonable to assume that she would make life more than a little uncomfortable for her. No, it was not wise to remain any longer than she must, decided Laura eventually, and the following morning she lost no time in seeking out the Conde and informing him of her decision.

'Leaving?' he repeated with a frown. 'Without finishing the job you came here to do?' He stared questioningly at her. 'Your reason, *senhorita*?'

'I feel homesick,' lied Laura, already having this excuse ready. 'I'll certainly finish those I've already started, as I've just said, but I don't want to start any more.'

The Conde, who was standing with his back to the

window of his study, frowned more heavily at her, as she stood just inside the door, twisting her hands nervously together.

'I'm completely at a loss,' he said in that accented voice which Laura found so attractive, 'as to why you have so suddenly become homesick. You did say that you had no relatives in your country?'

Laura nodded.

'That's correct,' she answered.

'In that case,' returned Dom Duarte imperiously, 'there is no valid reason for your wanting to leave me without carrying out the work which I assigned to you.' His eyes were hard, his mouth set in an inflexible line. 'I expect you to stay,' he said finally, and before she knew it Laura had said,

'Very well, Dom Duarte,' and found herself passing from his room into the wide corridor outside. She stood quite still, staring at the door she had just closed. Her heart was beating far too swiftly, her pulses were racing. She had gone in there with the firm intention of telling the Conde that she could not stay much longer at the Palacio; she had emerged without having succeeded ... but why? Dom Duarte could not force her to stay; she had a will of her own and she knew how to use it.

'There was something,' she murmured, moving away from the door in case he should open it and see her there. 'Yes, there was something ... which I could not understand.' His eyes had been hard ... yet not unkindly so. His mouth had been firm ... and yet she now realised that, subconsciously, she had expected it to relax in a smile. His voice was authoritative, imperious ... and yet, thinking about it now, Laura sensed an underlying quality of softness which he had deliberately tried to conceal. Did he love her? Certainly he felt something for her; she had already reached this conclusion. But he would never allow his emotions to triumph over his common sense. This conclusion had also been reached by Laura.

She went out into the garden, her mind so confused that she knew she could not find the necessary concentration to work on the pictures. So many conflicting thoughts and ideas flitted about in her mind, not least of which was the question: why did not the Conde welcome her decision to leave the Palacio? Surely her continued presence here must be upsetting him—if, of course, Laura's assumptions were correct and he did feel something for her. Better for his peace of mind if she were no longer living in his home.

She wandered on, into the Park, seeking the solitude she knew she would find there. But this was not to last long, for within a few minutes she heard the sound of hooves and, turning her head, she saw Dona Eduarda coming towards her. She was riding Ludran, but dismounted as she came alongside Laura.

'I thought you worked during the mornings?' were her first words, spoken with an almost virulent inflection. 'Does Dom Duarte know you're out here at this time?'

'No,' answered Laura stiffly, 'he doesn't.'

'Then why are you?' demanded Dona Eduarda arrogantly. 'If you don't get on with that work you're going to be here for ever.'

Laura coloured hotly, with temper. This was the kind of treatment she would receive when once this girl was established here as the mistress of the Palacio de Mauredo. However, she was not married to the Conde yet, therefore it was none of her business whether Laura was working in the Gallery or not.

'I fail to see what that has to do with you,' she returned, meeting the dark and narrowed eyes unflinchingly. 'You are not my employer, Dona Eduarda.'

'You're insolent!' The narrowed eyes became mere slits. Laura had the incredible impression that the Portuguese girl was jealous of her. 'I might as well tell you, Miss Conroy, that if I were your employer I'd have dismissed you long before now! You're lazy!'

Lazy ... Laura felt herself becoming inflamed, a most unusual experience for her, normally being so placid and good-tempered.

'You've just accused me of insolence,' she flashed, 'but it is you who are insolent!'

The girl drew a deep breath, making a sort of hissing sound. However, she had regained her self-composure by the time she spoke.

'It is beneath my dignity to bandy words with a mere servant,' she said, turning to mount the horse. 'I shall inform Dom Duarte that you are not working. I expect he will know how to deal with you.'

Laura watched her ride away, her whole body quivering with anger. How dared the girl speak to her like that! And to call her a servant! Dom Duarte himself had never done so; in fact, he was most emphatic that she was *not* a servant.

A quarter of an hour later Laura was walking across the lawn towards the Palacio when she saw Dona Eduarda and the Conde in conversation. They were standing on the front patio and neither of them noticed Laura. She made a diversion, taking a path round the side of the house, so when the Conde came up to the Gallery about ten minutes later Laura was in her blue nylon overall, a paintbrush in her hand.

'Ah, so you're busy, *senhorita*.'

She turned slowly, her lovely eyes examining his face for any sign of anger. She saw only an expressionless mask, but did note the tightness of his clenched fists.

Laura spoke stiffly, her eyes still fixed upon his face.

'I've only just started, as you are aware, Dom Duarte. So I shall work during the afternoon to make up.'

The Conde frowned at her.

'I believe I expressed the wish that you should not work during the afternoons,' he said.

'But I've only just started,' she repeated. And then, when he did not speak, she added defiantly, 'I expect Dona Eduarda told you that I was uncivil to her! Well, *senhor*, I am now telling you that I don't regret it! Please say what you have to say, but keep that in mind. I *do not regret it*!'

The Conde's eyes widened a little.

'Dona Eduarda was obviously uncivil to you, *senhorita*?'

'She was!'

'And what do you expect me to say to you—er—keeping in mind, as you instruct me to, that you do not regret being uncivil to Dona Eduarda?'

Laura looked bewilderingly at him, fully aware that there was no anger directed towards herself, and yet it did seem that anger lurked beneath the rather mild manner he was adopting. Incredibly, Laura had the idea that his anger was for Dona Eduarda!

'I expect I was prepared for some censure from you,' she told him perplexedly, 'but you are not angry with me, apparently?'

'Censure, eh? For not starting work on time, or for your incivility towards Dona Eduarda?'

Laura shrugged helplessly.

'You puzzle me, Dom Duarte,' she said.

'Yes, *senhorita*,' he returned much to her surprise, 'I expect I do,' and he added before she could speak, 'I am not thinking of censuring you. The work here will be done eventually and, as I told you at first, there is no particular hurry.' He paused a moment, his grey eyes regarding her with the most odd expression. Laura, the paintbrush still idle in her hand, wondered if it were her imagination, or if Dom Duarte's voice had carried a strange inflection when he had uttered the words, '... no particular hurry'. He spoke again, surprising her still further by saying, 'I am not intending to censure you for anything you said to Dona Eduarda. I feel you had some cause, *senhorita*.' The Conde paused, faintly amused by Laura's bewildered expression. 'Retaliation is often permissible,' he continued presently, 'if only because it is a natural instinct.'

So he knew more than he had revealed about Dona Eduarda's treatment of her, decided Laura, and her heart became light, her pulse behaving in the most unfamiliar way. She was aware of the colour fluctuating in her cheeks, of the fact that the smile on her lips would have affected her eyes. The Conde was looking into them, his own lips curved in a half-smile. She spoke, hesitantly and rather shyly.

'You are obviously more understanding than I ever imagined, *senhor*.'

His smile deepened.

'You're becoming braver, *senhorita*,' he said in some amusement. 'At one time you would not have had the temerity to speak to me like that.'

Laura gave a little laugh, much to her own surprise.

'You don't resent it, obviously.'

A small silence followed and Laura began to wonder if she had gone too far, adopting this familiarity with him. Yet he himself had started it by discarding that austere manner to which she was used. He had been human enough to understand just how she felt regarding Dona Eduarda; he had smiled at her in a way that encouraged a venturesome response. And what of his expression at this moment? So soft ... almost tender, that look in his eyes ...

'No,' he was saying quietly, 'I do not resent it.'

Laura glanced away, deeply affected by this dramatic change in him. She tried not to hazard a guess as to what it might mean, and yet her heart was racing, and unfamiliar vibrations rippled through her body. Memory brought back many occasions when his manner had puzzled her, when he had looked at her with admiration in his cool grey eyes. She looked at him, unconsciously imploring him to say something that would give her a lead as to his inner feelings, and what this attitude he was adopting towards her really meant. But when presently he did break the silence it was merely to say,

'I shall leave you to your task, *senhorita*. Remember, you do not work after lunch.'

She watched his tall aristocratic figure as he strode the length of the Gallery, noting the broad shoulders and narrow hips, the light athletic gait, the total silence of his footsteps on the thickly carpeted floor. A truly magnificent personage, this lord of the manor and virtual ruler of the island of Torassa.

Laura turned to her work, but her mind was on what had just transpired between the Conde and herself. She had expected to feel his anger, to be told coldly that she must not treat his guest with disrespect. Instead she had been told by the Conde that she had merely followed a natural instinct in retaliating to Dona Eduarda's own rudeness. How could he have guessed that the girl had been rude? wondered Laura, then immediately told herself that the Conde was no fool. His powers of perception were strong, she felt sure, and in any case, her own angry assertion that she did not regret her incivility would have been enough to give him a clue.

Feeling as she did, with her mind confused by the Conde's changed manner, Laura was by no means sorry when lunch time arrived and she was able to finish her work for the day. It was too difficult to concentrate, and she could only hope she would feel differently tomorrow.

Teresa brought her lunch up to her room, and Laura ate it on the verandah, in the sunshine, and with the delightful views of the Palacio gardens rolling away to the Great Park beyond. Gay parakeets noisily flew from tree to tree; brightly-coloured butterflies sought for nectar in the exotic blooms which grew in such profusion along the borders and on the parterres; the water-fowl on the lake added more colour by the brilliance of their plumage, as did the high fountain with its rainbow hues stolen from the sun.

A deep sigh escaped Laura as for some reason she could not dispel the picture of Dona Eduarda becoming mistress here. That there was little or no love between her and Dom Duarte was obvious to anyone with any intelligence at all, but would that matter so long as there was produced an heir to all this, and to the island of Torassa? Laura then thought of her own reaction to the Conde's very attractive mood of that morning. She had known a warmth, and an upsurge of the love she felt for him. Yearning had been strong within her and she now wondered if this had been reflected in her eyes. Still, the Conde would not have known what her expression meant. Keen as were his powers of perception were he could never have guessed that she was in love with him. No, for she had managed very well indeed to hide her feelings.

When Teresa came to clear away after Laura had had

her to lunch, the girl informed her that Dona Eduarda was leaving the Palacio later that afternoon.

'Leaving?' echoed Laura in disbelief. 'Are you sure, Teresa?'

'Yes, *senhorita*. My Martim is instructed to drive her to the airport.'

Laura shook her head in bewilderment.

'Martim? Is not Dom Duarte taking her there himself?' Laura knew this was not the kind of talk of which the Conde would approve; nevertheless, she was so intrigued by Teresa's information that her curiosity got the better of her.

'No, it is Martim who is taking her.'

Laura said no more, but as Teresa was leaving, the silver tray in her hands, she turned her head and said,

'I think that there will not now be a marriage between Dom Duarte and Dona Eduarda.'

Laura stared disbelievingly, profoundly conscious of her nerves rioting, her heart beating far more quickly than before.

'Not be a marriage ...?' Laura's words trailed off; Teresa had already passed through the doorway and was turning into the corridor. What had happened? And how had this information come to Teresa?

Laura, her mind in a turmoil, the result of a multitude of unanswerable questions darting through it, went from her room and down to the garden. There was no sign either of the Conde or his guest—only silence, deep and tranquil, over the beautiful gardens of the Palacio. Restless, Laura decided to pay a visit to Melanie and Pedro. A little light conversation over afternoon tea would provide the diversion which Laura needed.

Pedro was somewhere in the grounds, but Melanie

was there, and she greeted her visitor with a spontaneous and welcoming smile.

'What a pleasant surprise, Laura! Do come in—or perhaps you prefer the sunny outdoors?'

'Yes, I'm still thrilled with the sunshine, here on Torassa,' smiled Laura, watching Melanie beckon to one of the gardeners. He came instantly, was told to bring out two chairs.

'I believe Eduarda's here again,' said Melanie conversationally once she and Laura were seated.

'Yes, but Teresa told me she's leaving this afternoon.'

'Leaving?' Melanie's eyes opened wide. 'She's only just come, hasn't she?'

Laura nodded.

'She hasn't been here very long.'

'It's rumoured all over the island that she and Duarte would become engaged. Have they?' Melanie added as an afterthought.

'No.' Laura paused uncertainly, then decided not to repeat what Teresa had said about there not now being a marriage between the Conde and Dona Eduarda.

'Strange,' mused Melanie, clearly intrigued by the situation. 'They're so suited; but perhaps Duarte's a little piqued that Eduarda once passed him up for someone else.'

'I don't know how she could.' The words were out before Laura could stop them.

'You don't?' with a new interest. 'Not fallen for his handsome masculinity yourself, have you?' added Melanie with a laugh.

'Certainly not!'

'Very vehement. Not convincing.'

Laura frowned darkly at her.

'Does every girl who comes to Torassa fall in love with the Conde?' she asked, meaning to be sarcastic.

'Without exception. You must admit that he's something quite out of the ordinary.'

Laura changed the subject, asking if Melanie had heard from her brother recently.

'As a matter of fact I had a letter today; it came in on the plane which Eduarda's obviously taking. Rex says he'd like to come over before Christmas. His boss has agreed to let him have a fortnight off—without pay, of course, because it'll be extra to Rex's ordinary holidays.' She was looking curiously at Laura as she added, 'He's coming to see you, mainly, not us.'

Laura shook her head protestingly.

'Don't say such things, Melanie. I do hope Rex isn't cherishing any false hopes about him and me.'

'That he's cherishing hopes is an undoubted fact, I'm afraid.'

'Oh, dear,' sighed Laura with a frown. 'I'm sure I haven't given him any encouragement.'

'A man in love doesn't need it. He knows what he wants and sets out to get it.'

Plain speaking indeed. Laura was uncomfortable and again changed the subject.

'Do you and Pedro ever go for a holiday?'

'Now and again. Pedro doesn't find anywhere comparable to Torassa, so he says there's not much sense in leaving the island, not even for a couple of weeks or so. However, we have been to Portugal twice, just to visit Pedro's relatives.'

'Dom Duarte has relatives there, he's told me.'

'That's right. And of course Eduarda's home is there. She has a magnificent house which her husband left her.'

'Her husband must have died young?'

'It's Pedro's belief that Eduarda knew he had an incurable disease before she married him.'

Laura's eyes widened.

'You mean—she married him just to inherit his fortune?'

'That's what Pedro maintains. He hasn't any time for the girl and can never understand how Duarte could ever have been interested in her.'

'But you yourself consider them to be suited to one another?'

'I find them both coldly unemotional, and I do think that Eduarda's fortune would be of interest to Duarte, in spite of his own wealth. Pedro doesn't agree with me, either that Duarte is coldly unemotional or that he would be interested in Eduarda's money.'

'I feel that Pedro is right—if you'll forgive my saying so, Melanie.'

'You do?' Melanie looked curiously at her. 'So you are not of the opinion that he is unemotional?'

'I was at first, but not now.'

'And why, might I ask?'

Laura shrugged carelessly, feigning indifference.

'It's merely that, having got to know him better, I find certain traits which at first didn't appear to exist.'

'You seem to have been making a studied analysis of our friend,' observed Melanie in some amusement.

Laura coloured.

'No such thing. I'm not that interested.' She averted her head, conscious of the white lie she had told.

'Tell me,' invited Melanie, 'just what is your opinion of Duarte?'

'Of his character?'

'Of him as a person.'

'Well ... at first I thought him arrogant and rather full of his own importance. I regarded him in the light of a feudal lord, with all his vassals around him.' Laura's voice held a tinge of amusement. 'Now, how-

178

ever, I feel that he's merely proud of his ancestry, and that he regards himself most fortunate in owning this island.'

'In other words, he's now a likeable character—in your opinion, that is?'

Laura found herself nodding in agreement.

'He could be very attractive, I'm sure. And as for his being interested in Eduarda's wealth—I once believed he could be, but not now.'

Melanie's gaze was disconcerting, and it was with a sigh of relief that Laura saw Pedro come from the direction of a small secluded copse and stride across the lawn towards the place where they were sitting. He greeted Laura, then ordered tea to be served on the patio. An hour later Laura was leaving, having promised to pay another visit on the following Sunday afternoon.

The Conde had invited Laura to dine with him. She received the invitation with mixed feelings, aware that had Dona Eduarda been here then she, Laura, would not have been asked to dine at the Conde's table. However, she was happy to be having dinner with him, and she chose a particularly flattering dress of apple-green lace, its tight-fitting bodice accentuating her delicate curves. Nipped in at the waist, it then billowed out from a series of small pleats which widened towards the hemline. Laura brushed her hair until it shone, touched her lips with rouge, sparingly applied a delectable perfume, tucked a lace-edged handkerchief into the tight cuff of the dress, and then, after taking one last critical look at herself in the mirror, she went down to the room where she knew the Conde would be waiting for her. She stopped by the door, to stare at him, as he stood by the cocktail cabinet, his slim, athletic figure superbly attired in a white linen suit. He had turned his head, and their eyes met. A long unfathomable moment passed before Dom Duarte, a smile coming readily to his lips, invited her to sit down. He poured her a drink, then took possession of a chair opposite to her.

'May I say how very pretty that dress is, *senhorita*?'

She blushed rosily.

'Thank you, Dom Duarte,' she murmured, almost inaudibly. The window was wide open, allowing heady perfumes to invade the room. In one corner stood a huge Grecian-style urn full of glorious crimson flowers with a hidden light behind them so that shafts of amber pierced the spaces between the flower petals and the vivid green foliage. Wall lights were also throwing off an amber glow, but the light from the central chandelier was like a myriad diamonds twinkling all together.

The Conde chatted about the pictures; Laura realised at once that she knew she was feeling awkward and was in consequence easing the situation for her. Why she should feel awkward she did not know, unless it was owing to the amazing change in the Conde's attitude towards her, that morning, in the Gallery.

They went in to dinner, which was served by Gigo with his usual quiet efficiency. Candles lit the table, which gleamed with silver and rare porcelain. In a silver bowl roses of several colours were expertly arranged, while at Laura's cover was a single rose in a cut-glass holder. The perfume of the roses had drifted to her nostrils as she sat down and a smile leapt to her lips. Her eyes became moist and limpid, and unconsciously she raised them to the Conde, who was by her chair, having drawn it out for her. A tense moment ensued; she felt the Conde's hand touch her shoulder and knew it was done deliberately. She noticed a sudden movement in his throat, and then a smile came swiftly to his lips ... a smile that set her heart racing. She felt the colour come to her cheeks, was aware of Dom Duarte's indecision before, his smile deepening, he took possession of his own chair at the table.

During the meal it was plain to Laura that this was to be a momentous occasion. The Conde was so charming with her, so attentive, so concerned when, her nerves and her emotions having affected her appetite, he asked if the food was not to her liking. And when the meal was over he put his hand under her elbow in the most proprietorial manner as he led her into the Blue Lounge where Gigo was to serve them with their coffee. He left quietly; a long silence ensued and Laura sought almost frantically for something to say.

'Dona Eduarda left rather suddenly——' Laura broke off, disgusted with herself for her inability to find a more suitable subject for the occasion.

'She did,' returned Dom Duarte grimly. 'I requested her to leave today.'

Laura stared at him questioningly, but said nothing. Dom Duarte told her to drink her coffee, adding that they would then take a stroll in the garden. Her nerves quivered as an access of sheer happiness shot through her. No necessity for any more questions, for Dom Duarte's expression told her all she needed to know. He could not possibly look at her like this if he did not love her.

Ten minutes later they were standing by the fountain, its waters lit with a rose-coloured glow given off from some hidden source at its base. Dom Duarte spoke softly, taking her hand in his.

'You have guessed why I have brought you out here?' He glanced up automatically to the deep purple sky where a crescent moon shone among a million stars.

'It's—it's—romantic,' she stammered absurdly, her fascinated gaze fixed upon his fingers as they caressed the back of her hand.

Dom Duarte smiled in some amusement.

'Romantic enough for a proposal of marriage, do you think?'

'I d-don't know wh-what to say ...' The faltering words trailed away as Dom Duarte put out his other hand and drew her to his breast; and with an infinite tenderness he tilted her face so that he could claim her lips.

'My darling,' he murmured when presently he held her from him. 'I love you very dearly.'

Laura said nothing, for emotion was deep and strong, preventing speech. She had thrilled to his kiss, yet was conscious of a strange disappointment. The Conde had not revealed the warmth she had subconsciously desired, had in fact seemed unable to show any depth of emotion. But, quite suddenly, and certainly unexpectedly, his ardour came forth unrestrainedly and she was drawn into a whirlpool of passion that almost robbed her of her senses. She felt his hard demanding mouth force her lips apart, knew the possessive caress of his hand as it touched the tender curve of her breast, was vitally aware of his hard body against hers, coercing her to relax the tautness of her own slender frame. A sort of wild ecstasy engulfed her and she surrendered to his demands, carried helplessly on the tide of his passion. Helplessly ... but willingly, and a laugh of tender triumph mingled with the music of the fountain when once again Laura was held at arms' length.

'You—angel! Laura, how has this come about? How can you have fallen in love with anyone like me——? Oh, yes, I have known for some time,' he added when it seemed she would venture a surprised inquiry. 'Your lovely eyes have many times revealed what is in your heart.' Laura coloured almost painfully at the idea of allowing her feelings to be read, especially at a time when—she supposed—*he* had not yet fallen in love with *her*. 'You said that I puzzled you,' he went on gently. 'You see, Laura, I had given Eduarda to understand that I would marry her, and as a gentleman who has always honoured his word, I had the greatest difficulty in extricating myself from my promise.' He paused a moment, considering. 'Do you remember that morning when you came to me in the garden, to tell me you couldn't accept the replacement of the clothes you'd spoiled?'

'Yes, I remember.' Starry-eyed, she looked up at him. 'You were so very different. You asked me to stay and keep you company.'

'That's right. Until then I'd been fighting against my growing love for you, thinking only of my honour and my obligation towards Eduarda. But that morning ...' His voice became very soft and tender as he continued, 'I knew, my dearest, that it was not possible for me to marry anyone but you.'

'Oh ...!' Laura stared at him with an expression of comical dismay. 'Do you know what I thought when I heard you say that?'

'Say what?'

'The words, "not possible".'

'No.' He looked perplexedly at her.

'I thought you'd come to care for me but had decided it was not possible for you to marry me, because of the great difference in our positions.'

He frowned down at her.

'You believed I'd allow that to influence me?'

'Well ...'

'Never, my dear. I wanted to kiss you that morning——'

'I knew it!' interrupted Laura with a sort of triumph. 'Oh, Dom Duarte, I wish you had! You have no idea how miserable I've been ...' She tailed off, seeing the glimmer of amusement that lit his eyes. 'What's so funny?' she asked, wondering at her confidence. 'It was no laughing matter.'

'I was amused by your mode of address, my love. I do think that as we are to be married within the next week or so you can drop the title, don't you?'

She gave a shaky laugh.

'It will be difficult, at first, for me to call you—call you—Duarte.'

'Will it?' he asked teasingly. 'Well, practice will make a difference.'

Laura gave another laugh; Duarte seemed fascinated by her lovely eyes, and by the quivering of her softly-parted lips. With a swift possessive gesture he drew her against him, claiming her lips in a long and ardent kiss. Laura, though giving herself up to the delights of the moment, was, nevertheless, waiting for Duarte to tell her more about his relationship with Dona Eduarda. This he did, presently, and Laura learned that the marriage had actually been desired by both his parents and Eduarda's. But she had married someone else, and Duarte had not been in any way put out simply because, had he himself married Eduarda, it would merely have been a marriage of convenience.

'A man in my position wants an heir,' he continued unemotionally, 'and Eduarda would have made a suitable wife for me. When her husband died we again discussed marriage and decided that when a suitable period of time had elapsed we would then come together——'

'But surely you wanted some warmth, some affection,' protested Laura, quite unable to help interrupting him. To her surprise he shook his head.

'Until I met you, Laura, there had never been any thought of love. Eduarda is beautiful; she is of nobility, and so she was suited to my—er—requirements——' He stopped, this time interrupting himself. 'Enough of that,' he said with a frown. And as he looked down into Laura's eyes a great wave of tenderness resulted in his voice becoming husky. 'You, my little English rose, made me realise that life without love is worthless. Thank you, my darling, for coming to this island.'

Laura tried to speak, but failed because of the lump in her throat. This was sheer bliss, and silence seemed to suit the atmosphere of drowsy gardens beneath the tropical sky, of exotic perfumes of the breeze, of music from the cascading waters of the fountain. There was no need for speech, and Laura nestled comfortably against Duarte's breast, and put her hand upon his shoulder. She felt possessive ... and yet exceedingly meek and helpless. After a long while Duarte said,

'What are you thinking, my beloved?'

She had just thought of that incident in the sea and without hesitation she replied,

'I'm thinking about something that has puzzled me for a while, Duarte. That day Clara went into the sea——'

'I had intended coming to that,' was Duarte's grim interruption. 'For some time I'd had my doubts, hence the questions I put to you. You weren't the type of girl to leave Clara to drown; this I soon admitted to myself. And having done so I set about trying to learn the truth.' He stopped and looked sternly at her. 'You yourself were determined not to enlighten me, so I attempted to get something out of Clara, but she was vague about what had happened——'

'Which was understandable,' broke in Laura. 'Please go on,' she pressed.

'When you went into that bog after Clara I had the proof I wanted, but that meant that Eduarda had deliberately lied, which didn't seem feasible——' Again he stopped and his mouth became compressed. 'I related to Eduarda what had happened in the bog, saying that your action on that occasion did not fit in at all with the fact that you had previously left my niece to drown.' Duarte paused, his eyes narrowing. 'I saw at once that Eduarda had lied over that incident in the sea. She gave herself away by her obvious uneasiness, so I tackled her. She admitted to telling a deliberate lie.' Again he paused, but when Laura remained silent he added, 'And so I had an excuse for telling Eduarda that I was not now going to marry her.'

'She took your decision mildly?'

'She accepted it, and agreed to leave Torassa. However, she had guessed that I was in love with you and she made that stupidly childish attempt to cause dissension between us by reporting that you weren't at your work in the Gallery.' Duarte frowned as he ended, a sign that he considered the topic unworthy of any further waste of time. And as Laura was in full agreement she lifted her face invitingly and Duarte, his eyes dark with emotion, bent his head to take what she was so eagerly offering.

'My darling!' His lips were hard, almost ruthlessly demanding. 'I never dreamed I'd meet a girl like you!'

'Nor I a man like you,' rejoined Laura shakily when at length she was released. 'Oh, Duarte, I hope I shan't let you down——'

Duarte shook her, but gently.

'Don't you dare say anything like that again! You could never let me down, not in any way at all!'

'No ...' The catch in her voice, caused by his stern tones, was not lost on him and he instantly brought her to his heart again.

'Sweet ...' he murmured softly, 'I didn't mean to hurt you.' And he kissed her, gently this time, and when presently she looked up into his eyes she saw the infinite tenderness contained in them.

'You will never hurt me,' she returned with confidence. 'Nor I you, dearest Duarte,' she added lovingly as, putting her arms around his neck, she went up on tiptoe and pressed her lips to his.

Did you miss any of these exciting Harlequin Omnibus 3-in-1 volumes?

Anne Hampson

Anne Hampson #3
Heaven Is High (#1570)
Gold Is the Sunrise (#1595)
There Came a Tyrant (#1622)

Essie Summers

Essie Summers #6
The House on Gregor's Brae (#1535)
South Island Stowaway (#1564)
A Touch of Magic (#1702)

Margaret Way

Margaret Way #2
Summer Magic (#1571)
Ring of Jade (#1603)
Noonfire (#1687)

Margaret Malcolm

Margaret Malcolm #2
Marriage by Agreement (#1635)
The Faithful Rebel (#1664)
Sunshine on the Mountains (#1699)

Eleanor Farnes

Eleanor Farnes #2
A Castle in Spain (#1584)
The Valley of the Eagles (#1639)
A Serpent in Eden (#1662)

Kay Thorpe

Kay Thorpe
Curtain Call (#1504)
Sawdust Season (#1583)
Olive Island (#1661)

18 magnificent Omnibus volumes to choose from:

Betty Neels

Betty Neels #3
Tangled Autumn (#1569)
Wish with the Candles (#1593)
Victory for Victoria (#1625)

Violet Winspear

Violet Winspear #5
Raintree Valley (#1555)
Black Douglas (#1580)
The Pagan Island (#1616)

Anne Hampson

Anne Hampson #4
Isle of the Rainbows (#1646)
The Rebel Bride (#1672)
The Plantation Boss (#1678)

Margery Hilton

Margery Hilton
The Whispering Grove (#1501)
Dear Conquistador (#1610)
Frail Sanctuary (#1670)

Rachel Lindsay

Rachel Lindsay
Love and Lucy Granger (#1614)
Moonlight and Magic (#1648)
A Question of Marriage (#1667)

Jane Arbor

Jane Arbor #2
The Feathered Shaft (#1443)
Wildfire Quest (#1582)
The Flower on the Rock (#1665)

Great value in reading at $2.25 per volume

Joyce Dingwell

Joyce Dingwell #3
Red Ginger Blossom (#1633)
Wife to Sim (#1657)
The Pool of Pink Lilies (#1688)

Hilary Wilde

Hilary Wilde
The Golden Maze (#1624)
The Fire of Life (#1642)
The Impossible Dream (#1685)

Flora Kidd

Flora Kidd
If Love Be Love (#1640)
The Cave of the White Rose (#1663)
The Taming of Lisa (#1684)

Lucy Gillen

Lucy Gillen #2
Sweet Kate (#1649)
A Time Remembered (#1669)
Dangerous Stranger (#1683)

Gloria Bevan

Gloria Bevan
Beyond the Ranges (#1459)
Vineyard in a Valley (#1608)
The Frost and the Fire (#1682)

Jane Donnelly

Jane Donnelly
The Mill in the Meadow (#1592)
A Stranger Came (#1660)
The Long Shadow (#1681)

Complete and mail this coupon today!